The Crystal Rose

by

Francis Eugene Wood

Special thanks to

Elizabeth Pickett
for her editing skills and advice;
my wife, Chris,
for her patience and encouragement;
and a stranger
for a kind manner and an unselfish offering.

Published by Tip-of-the-Moon Publishing Co.
Farmville, Virginia
Printed by Farmville Printing
Photograph by Chris Wood
Book design by F.E.W.
All rights reserved
E-mail address: fewwords@moonstar.com
Web Site (http://tipofthemoon.com)
First U.S. Printing

ISBN: 0-9657047-3-4

In Loving Memory

of

Margaret Camden Wood

Table of Contents

– FOREWORD –

Some years ago I was given a very special gift. It was not given to me by a relative or by a friend or even by an acquaintance. Instead, it was offered to me by a stranger who asked but one question: "Do you dream?"

The gift was awesome in its beauty, and for the longest time I wondered about its meaning.

Then one night I fell asleep while holding it next to my pillow. That night I had a dream so real that I was sure I had lived it or at least been there in some way.

The following day I recorded the dream in my journal, just as it had come to me. More dreams followed, and every day I wrote them down. For seven days I awoke tired, yet somehow fulfilled in my heart and soul.

Although these dreams were different, there was one thing that appeared in each one. It was the gift I had been given by the stranger -- a crystal rose in a wooden box. . . .

The Drunkard

Elias Bleeksteen was a man in trouble. He had lost everything. There was nothing left of the life he had built, or so he thought. And worst of all there was no one to blame but himself. A drunkard always needs someone to blame. That is his nature. A lowdown scoundrel of a scapegoat is all he needs to justify his pathetic state of being. Elias could not come up with even one scoundrel. Instead, he cursed himself as he buried his face in his hands.

The cold November rain now drenched his hunched shoulders. Elias was not aware of it; he was too absorbed in guilt and grief. And there was anger in him, intense anger, which caused him to reach his hands upwards and shout, "What have I done? Oh, God! What have I done?" There was no answer from heaven. All that Elias Bleeksteen heard was the rain that pelted his face.

He walked on aimlessly, past the lighted places of town into dark alleys where he might be clubbed on the head and killed and so be relieved of his misery. But there was no other person out on that night. Elias tried his best to coax a hoodlum from a shadow. "Come on, damn you!" he slurred. "I've still some money, here!" He withdrew a few crumpled bills from his coat pocket and flapped them in the rain. "Come on out and kill me, and you can have it all!" he cried. Elias waited, but nothing happened, so he stuffed the soggy bills back in his coat pocket and mumbled, "Where are the hoodlums when you need them?"

He stumbled out of an alley and on to the sidewalk, where the lights from town reflected in the shop windows. He leaned against a lamp post to steady himself, and then the lights began to swirl around him. His last thought before awakening in a coach on the street outside his home was that Main Street looked like a glistening river and he wished he could drown in it.

He had not drowned. Instead, he heard a voice say, "Elias, it's time to go home to your wife."

Elias, wet and miserable, opened his eyes and looked at the face of a man he knew. "Linden," he sighed, "where am I? What happened?"

The big man shook his head and answered, "You passed out on the street, Elias. You could have been killed tonight." Linden Sharkley turned in his seat and picked at the reins he held between his fingers. "Can you walk to the door, or do you need help?" His tone was stern.

Elias stared through the rain at his house. He could see a dim light in the sitting room.

She was there now, waiting, the woman who should have left him long ago, the woman who had always been there for him, who had given him two beautiful children, a boy and a girl. Her name was Natalie, but Elias had always called her Nattie.

Elias fumbled for his pocket watch and tilted it towards the street light to see the time. He shook his head. The children would have been in bed for hours by now, and Nattie --

"She is worried sick about you, Elias." Linden broke the silence with a voice thick with concern.

"I cannot go in, Linden," answered Elias. "It would break my heart to see her after what I've done." He placed the watch back in his vest pocket and rubbed his brow with his fingers. He could not look into the face of his friend, but he felt the man's eyes on him and they burned him. They burned him, not because they condemned him, but because he condemned himself. A tear trickled down Elias' face as he spoke. "I lost it all tonight, Linden."

"You lost your money?" questioned the big man.

"No. I lost what was left of that last week." Elias swallowed hard and forced himself to voice the rest. "Tonight I lost the jewelry store."

Linden Sharkley could not believe his ears, and for a moment he said nothing. He stared into the rain. His mind was reaching for the right words, but he simply could not speak.

He recalled the day, ten years earlier, when Elias and Nattie first arrived in town.

They were so full of life and dreams. She dreamt of a home and children. He dreamt of a successful business and respect in the community. And they had it all. The perfect life, it seemed, and perhaps they believed it was so. But it wasn't perfect. Nothing ever is. Maybe it was that realization that caused Elias to drift away from his wife, even from his children. What is it that can make a man turn away from the love of his family? The reasons are many and complex, for so often they come from within.

Linden thought that perhaps it was the pressure Elias had put on himself to succeed. And what was Elias' barometer of success? How did he see himself? Linden Sharkley could only wonder. He had tried to talk to his friend, but he could not reach him. There were barriers to their conversations and too little sharing of their lives. Instead, he'd ask, "Why, Elias?" or "How can you drink and gamble away your life, Elias?" The answers lay somewhere in the silence of his troubled friend. Linden would come away feeling sad and defeated. No one wants to fail a friend.

Even though Linden had kept his distance from Elias, he could not help loving him and Nattie and the children. It was for them that he would go out on nights like this and leave his own wife and children alone, always hoping it would be the last time he would need to go.

A dog barked, and Linden fidgeted in his seat. "Go into your house, Elias," he pleaded.

"I cannot," came the answer.

Linden looked hard at his pathetic friend, and he reached into his breast pocket and brought out a pencil and half of an old envelope.

He pushed them into Elias' hands and said, "Write a note to Nattie and tell her that you have gambled away the store and that your life no longer belongs to you."

Elias stared at Linden in disbelief. He could not speak. He tried to say "No," but he could not utter a word.

Linden continued, "Tell her that you now belong to the bottle and the gamblers and the whores!" He turned his head and spat in disgust, then resumed his verbal onslaught. "Tell her to hold your children at night and kiss them, for you are too weak and your tongue is ragged with lies! Tell her there is no love left in your heart and that you would rather lie cold and alone in the streets than to feel the warmth of her caress."

Elias could take it no longer. He wailed and covered his ears, but the words echoed in his mind. He was mad with shame and degradation, and where his voice failed him, his fists prevailed. He struck out and landed a blow that caught Linden just below his right eye. The big man was knocked off guard and tumbled out of his seat and into the rain-puddled road. The horse lurched forward with fright as Linden stumbled to his feet and grabbed for the reins. At the same time, Elias leapt upon him, pummeling his head and shoulders with blows and shouting,

"No!"

Linden could have stopped him. He could have taken Elias' small fists in his hands and driven him to his knees. But he did not. Instead, he stood there until Elias' strength gave out. Then, while grasping the big man's coat, Elias slipped to his knees, a wretch of a man.

Someone else might have struck back at Elias that night or at least walked away from him. But not Linden Sharkley. He stood there, his face stained from the blood of his wounds and said softly, "If you cannot write those words, Elias, then perhaps there is hope for you." He reached down and with his strong hands pulled his friend to his feet.

Elias buried his face on the chest of the big man and wept like a child.

Linden calmed him. "Elias, you began a journey and have come to a bad place in your path." He put his arms around the trembling man and patted his back. "You might have thought you had seen the end of your journey, but I think you still have yet to arrive. Come, I will take you to the store, where you can pull yourself together."

As Elias stepped up onto the coach, he turned back. "But what about Nattie?"

"I will tell her you are all right," Linden

assured him. "And I will tell her where you are." He paused, then took the reins in his hand and urged the horse forward. "The rest," he said, "will be up to you, Elias."

Elias looked back at his home, and as the coach turned down another street, he saw the light in the room go out.

Later that night, Elias Bleeksteen sat alone at his desk and contemplated the events that had brought him there. Linden was right. He was at a bad place in his life. He looked through his office window, into the narrow, but tidy, jewelry store he had built, and his heart was heavy with regret. He had a week to turn it over to its new owner. How could he explain it, he wondered. Elias opened a desk drawer and felt for the bottle he knew was there. He closed the drawer and set the bottle on the desk in front of him. The light from the small oil lamp played on the whiskey sloshing back and forth inside the half-empty container. He watched it until it became settled. With one hand he opened the bottle and brought the cap to his nose. The smell of the whiskey enticed him at first, and he almost took a drink. Then he thought about something Linden had said to him, "You still have yet to arrive."

Elias returned the cap to the bottle and pushed himself away from the desk. "Arrive where?" he asked aloud.

He walked the narrow aisles of his shop, and by the lights of the street outside, he could see things, beautiful things. Some were imported, and others were bought from salesmen. But the most wonderful items in the store were those he had designed and made himself. He stopped at a shelf near the front of the store and reached for a glistening crystal object. It was intended to be a fairy princess, but his children said it was an angel. Elias held the little piece up and studied it against the outside lights. It was a superb piece, he thought. Cut in a dance pose, the little fairy had wings rimmed in gold.

The man smiled when he thought of the work he had put into it. And he remembered it came from nothing. That was often the case when he cut crystal. Each piece would present itself as he worked. There was such satisfaction in it, he remembered. Elias smiled. His craftsmanship was what had brought him to this town. His proficiency at the art had supplied the capital for his venture into entrepreneurship. The smile slowly left his face as he tried to remember how long ago he had created the little fairy princess.

As Elias moved to the back of the store, the rain outside intensified, and the wind brought it hard against the store window. But Elias did not notice the rain or the wind. He did not even notice the bottle sitting in the lamplight on his desk as he walked past it and opened a door that led into his small workshop. He walked directly to his work table and lit a lamp. Anxiously, he opened a drawer and searched for something. The drawer was full of glass. There were pieces that were various sizes and shapes, but there was only one Elias wanted, and when he found it at the back of the drawer, he sighed. "There you are," he said softly, as he unfolded the felt cloth in which he had wrapped the piece several years before. He held it carefully in his hands and lifted it up to the light. Elias smiled as he viewed the shapeless piece of crystal, for he knew in his heart that something beautiful would be born of it that night.

He had known that feeling before as a young man. It had taken him to Germany, where he served as an apprentice to the masters for ten years. He had known the skilled craftsmen who turned molten glass into works of art. The dexterity of the blowers, the cutters, and the engravers was no secret to him.

So, when Elias began his task that night, he returned unto himself. His nature was to be creative. He had lost that vision of his true calling and had tried to become something he was not.

But that cold and rainy November night, as Elias worked with the tools of his trade, he began to feel as though he had somehow resumed a journey he had quit years ago. He smiled and nodded as he remembered the words of his friend, Linden Sharkley.

His skilled hands worked meticulously as he cut and sanded and buffed the glass piece into the object of his desire. Gone was the trembling of his hands. Instead, they were steady, and his precision with his tools was such that each movement was one of perfection.

Elias had always admired the crystal piece he worked with that night, for it was so unusual. It had caught his eye from the moment he had seen it. It was not without imperfections, but someone had added colors to it in its molten stage and the colors, a mixture of bright burgundy and a hint of emerald green, with a thin strand of rust running through its center, had made this piece stand out. For this reason Elias had set the piece apart from the others. "There is something in there," he had once said, and he had wrapped it and stored it in a safe place, with the intention of bringing out its secret one day. Little had he known it would take so long to get back to it. But Elias was back, and with each shaping of the crystal, he smiled and was pleased.

His work took him the rest of the night, and not once during that time did he think of the bottle on his desk. He thought of his work, and during the night, when he would push back from his work table to stretch and rest his eyes, he thought of Nattie and the children.

It was Sunday morning when Elias finished his task. When he held the small object in the palm of his hand and gazed at its beauty, he was overwhelmed with a feeling of accomplishment. He had brought out the mystery of the glass, and its beauty was beyond anything he could have imagined. It was born of his heart. Elias whispered, "Yes." Then he closed his eyes and spoke silently.

He walked to the front of the shop and was surprised to see that the rain had turned to snow during the night and had already cushioned the streets and sidewalks. As Elias raised the crystal object to the light of day and examined it, the grandfather clock at the back of the shop struck nine. He marveled once more at what had been a strangely colored piece of glass. Now it was a uniquely crafted work of art.

Elias smiled. "I uncovered your mystery and rediscovered myself," he said softly. "Now, I shall find you a safe place, so that your beauty will not be destroyed." Elias rummaged around in a drawer filled with empty boxes until he came across just the right one. It was a small walnut case with a dark satin inner cushion. Elias' eyes glistened as he placed the crystal object in the case and noticed how perfectly it fit. He closed the lid and placed the box in his pocket, just as a knock came at the front of the store.

Elias wondered who it might be on such a snowy Sunday morning, but as he approached the door, he saw it was the one person he needed most.

"Nattie," he said as he opened the door and pulled her close to him. No words were spoken at first, for in her caress there was love. Elias gently kissed her forehead and said almost in a whisper, "I have been such a fool, my love, and I can only say that I am sorry." There were tears in his eyes when Nattie touched his trembling lips with her fingers and spoke.

"Neither I nor our children need a jewelry store, Elias. It is not position or wealth that is important to us. But we do need you."

Elias could not hold back his emotion and lowering his face in her hands, he wept.

Moments passed, and when finally Elias could speak, he reached in his pocket and brought out the narrow wooden box. He offered it to his wife and said, "I made this last night, Nattie, when I thought that my life was ruined."

Nattie opened the lid and looked inside. Her eyes sparkled as she gently lifted the beautiful object from its resting place. "A crystal rose," she said.

Elias held his breath in anticipation.

Nattie examined the rose, noticing its cutting and clarity and the uniqueness of its coloring. She knew that its beauty had come from within her husband.

The crystal rose was a single half-opened bloom, whose burgundy petals were caressed by emerald leaves. A thin strand of rust was its stem, and it lay between the pages of a clear crystal book, where, upon one page, Elias had inscribed the word "Love."

The woman looked into the face of her husband and said the word.

Tears welled in Elias' eyes as he spoke from his heart. "It is the only thing that can save me, Nattie."

Nattie held the crystal rose to her breast with one hand and with the other stroked the cheeks of the man she had given her heart to so many years ago. "At this moment, Elias, I love you more than I ever have, for not only have you found yourself, but you have returned to me and our children."

Outside that day the snow continued to fall, and the wind blew. People carried on with their daily lives and were oblivious for the most part to the trials of others. But the love between Elias and Nattie Bleeksteen was made strong again that day, and as they stood in their quiet embrace, the only thing between their hearts was the crystal rose.

Some years later, in a city far away, Nattie Bleeksteen did something, the results of which neither she nor her late husband could ever have imagined. She began a journey. It was not a physical journey, for Nattie did not care much for travel. It was a journey of self-discovery that would profoundly affect the lives of other people, people whom she did not even know.

Nattie decided to give away the crystal rose. She knew in her heart that Elias would have understood. She could have kept it for years and passed it down through the family, but then it would have been cherished and guarded out of sentiment, its beauty unseen by others. Elias' gift should be shared, she thought, for was it not born of one who had come to the realization that love, the smallest word, was yet the greatest power of man?

The beauty of the crystal rose and the simplicity of the word on a page had somehow trans-formed one man's tragedy into a new beginning. Perhaps it would do the same for others.

So when Nattie gave away her beautiful treasure, she had but one request: "Understand its beauty and pass it on." It was a fair request, for once you have possessed the crystal rose, you will forever have its gift.

Brothers-in-Arms

Captain John Westing could hardly believe his good fortune. So much had happened in the past two years. First, he had graduated from West Point; then there was his appointment as attaché to General William L. Tinsley, who held court with some of the toughest officers in the U.S. Army.

Tiring of the political scene in Washington, John requested and received orders to serve under Major General William R. Shafter in what everyone agreed would be a quick victory in Cuba.

The year was 1898, and on the 15th of

April, John Westing could barely keep his seat by the window as his train pulled into the station in Richmond, Virginia. Seven days' leave would give him just enough time to marry the love of his life and honeymoon at his father's estate near Williamsburg, then join his fellow troops in Newport News.

As he stepped off the train and made his way through passengers and porters, he caught sight of a young woman who seemed to be looking for someone. He stood still for a moment and enjoyed her profile. Exquisitely dressed in the latest fashion, she was slim, but well-proportioned in a way that a young gentleman would appreciate. Her hair was dark and pinned neatly beneath a big chiffon hat. Her cheekbones were set high, and her eyes were as dark as midnight, with eyelashes to sweep the clouds. Her olive skin lent a softness to her face. When suddenly she spotted him in the crowd, the young officer smiled and moved quickly towards her.

"Oh, John!" she exclaimed. "I feared you had missed your train in Washington." She pulled back from his embrace and looked at him from head to toe. Then she smiled and said, "You are the most handsome gentleman in Richmond, Captain Westing."

John felt himself blush, but he enjoyed the

compliment even if Elizabeth Sharkley was somewhat prejudiced. "I am flattered that you would believe so, my dear; and for my own sake, I shall not question your lack of attention to the world around you."

They both laughed.

"Come, John, the carriage is waiting. Mother and Father will be so happy to see you." Elizabeth took his arm, and together they made their way through the station and to the carriage. The ride through the city was lovely, and John was impressed that so many finely dressed ladies and gentlemen greeted his future bride by name as they passed. His pride in Elizabeth was immense, for she was without a doubt the only woman who had ever captured his heart so completely that, when there was the slightest lull in his duties, he thought only of her and their life together.

He looked at her now, and she was more beautiful than he had remembered. "I have counted the days, Elizabeth." He held her hand and felt a surge of excitement move through his body.

"And I, also," she responded. "It is a circus at the house, and hardly a chair to sit upon," she laughed.

"We'll get through it just fine, my dear," he

assured her.

The wedding was quite an affair. It seemed that all of Richmond attended. But as weddings go, it was over quickly, and three days after Captain John Westing pulled into the Richmond train station, he lay upon a blanket beneath a giant oak tree on a bluff overlooking the James River.

The day was beautiful, and the newness of spring was evident everywhere. Songbirds chased each other in response to one another's calls. A slight breeze rustled the young leaves of oaks and maples and cooled the forehead of the new bride.

Elizabeth Sharkley Westing covered herself with her shawl and brought a glass of wine to her lips. She drank slowly, then touched the wine with her finger and wet the lips of her husband. He smiled lazily, without opening his eyes. Elizabeth looked at his face and knew, as she had known when she first met him, that she would love only this man for the rest of her life. She lay down beside him, her face on his chest, and listened to his heartbeat. Slow and steady, it was like the life she imagined they would have together.

A mourning dove cooed in the evergreens surrounding the yard, and suddenly Elizabeth was overcome with emotion. A tear fell across the bridge of her nose, and she wiped it away with her thumb.

"I love you, Elizabeth," John said, as he gently stroked her temple and smelled the cleanness of her hair.

Elizabeth sat up.

John opened his eyes and saw that she was tearful. He touched her elbow and asked, "What is it, darling?"

"You must promise me something, John," she responded.

"What?" His tone was serious.

There was so much she wanted to say, but her fear would not allow her to speak her thoughts. So she said only this: "Promise me that if ever you're afraid, you will think of me and imagine my embrace." She stopped for a moment and joined hands with her husband, then added, "I will be with you every minute of every day, my love. Until you come back to me."

John raised up and kissed her trembling lips. "I promise, Elizabeth," he said softly.

She bit her lip, and he pulled her to him. Off in the pines, the doves cooed. A fish broke the surface of an eddy below the bluff where spiders played ever so lightly across the water. Young leaves danced in the breeze, and birds continued to sing their songs. Everything had its purpose and acted and responded in accordance with its nature.

And high on a bluff above the river, two young lovers whispered promises and made plans for the future. . . .

Two months after his marriage to Elizabeth, Captain John Westing found himself at a table on foreign ground and in the presence of officers planning a battle. It was to be a two-pronged, full-scale assault upon a heavily fortified stone structure at a place called El Caney. The United States was at war with Spain, and Cuba was the battleground.

On the night of June 30th, John found a place away from his fellow officers where he could put his thoughts on paper in the form of a letter to his beloved wife.

In his mind he could see her on the grounds of his father's estate, walking alone or sitting at the oak tree near the bluff. Time had moved so quickly since the wedding.

John paused in his writing and recalled his departure for Florida. At the train station in Williamsburg, he held Elizabeth in his arms and told her of his love for her. He repeated his promises and dried her tears. He remembered that his wife had never looked more beautiful.

John reached into his breast pocket and retrieved a small wooden box. He smiled as he recalled the moment she had given it to him. It was just before he stepped onto the train. "I want you to have something," she had said. She took his hands and placed in them the wooden box.

"What is it, Elizabeth?" he questioned.

"My father gave it to me when I was a young girl," she replied. "It was given to him by the wife of his best friend."

John peered into the box. His eyes opened wide, and he took a quick breath. "Elizabeth!" he said. "It is so beautiful and delicate. I fear it will break."

"The box will protect it, darling. I want you to keep it with you always and look at it when you can. There is something about it."

John touched its burgundy petals with his finger and read the inscription on the clear page of the book. "Love," he said. "It is a beautiful rose, my dear. Thank you."

Elizabeth touched the face of her husband and kissed his lips. "I have looked upon this crystal rose for years, John, and its unique beauty, with the single word inscribed on the page, has lifted my spirits, and I am somehow able to see and feel the love around me." Elizabeth closed the wooden box in her husband's hands and pressed it against his chest. "Take the crystal rose, my love, and when you are alone or troubled, look at it and say the word and you, also, will feel its awesome power. Love, John. It is so simple and pure, yet to know it, moves us beyond the pain and strife of this world."

John knew his wife's words were from her heart, and when he finally waved goodbye to her at the station, he thanked God that she would be the mother of his child.

Captain John Westing folded his letter and sealed it carefully in an envelope. He wrote Elizabeth's name and address on the front of it and placed it in the mail bag.

Two days later, on July 1st, John led his men through a stream below San Juan Hill. His orders had been to ford the stream and take up position against the hill defenses. The plan was simple enough; however, there were so many troops that John's underlying feeling was no one was really in charge of anything.

An explosion ripped into the troops midway through the ford, cutting down scores of them. John shouted to his men to follow him, and he rushed towards the bank of the stream. The smell of muck and blood filled his nostrils, and he fell over the body of a soldier lying dead in knee-deep water. As John rose to his feet, another explosion in front of him sent him reeling backwards, slamming him into his own men. Stunned, the young captain watched as exploding shrapnel and enemy bullets tore into the troops, who were now in total chaos.

The stream had turned red, and John pulled himself up from the torn bodies around him and called to his men to rally again towards the stream bank. As he stumbled ahead, it was as if the gates of hell had opened. Smoke was thick and acrid and burned his eyes, but he could still see. He saw the soldier in front when his head exploded into a cloud of blood and smoke. The first lieutenant next to him was hit in the chest by a volley of bullets just as he stepped up onto the muddy bank, out of the bloody ford. As he fell, he grabbed his captain's arm, and John fell with him, his face just above the dying man. The lieutenant tried to speak, but in an instant John saw the life go out of his eyes.

John rose again and took several steps before the percussion from a nearby explosion slammed him again to the ground. Shaking his head, he focused his sight on a fallen tree and began to crawl towards it. Enemy fire was raking the ground around him when he felt his body being hoisted and then carried roughly to the safety of the tree and thrown onto the soft ground behind it. When he turned on his side and strained his eyes, he saw the face of a black soldier. "Sorry I'z so rough wit' ya, suh!" the soldier shouted. "But I fig'ud we best hurry on up dat bank."

"Thank you, soldier," John called out.

"Sho, suh."

"What's your name, soldier?"

"Name's Private Little Ben Moses, suh," answered the wide-eyed man. He ducked his head when a bullet hit the log near him. Tree bark spattered his sweating face, and he spit it off his lips. "Lawd knows, suh," he laughed. "We done got ourselves in a fix, all right, I reckon." Little Ben squinted his eyes. "Look at all dem boys dead in dat wut'uh."

John looked, but what he saw was a wagon sitting in mid-stream with a dead driver slumped over its side and two wild-eyed mules about ready to bolt. He raised his head and spied a good place up the hill where a few of his men had huddled.

"How would you like a wagon ride up that hill, Little Ben?" he shouted.

The large man smiled and nodded his head. "Dat's a Gatlin' gun, suh."

"You're damned right it is, soldier!"

"Din, let's git at it, suh, a'fo' dem boys up

'ar blow it ta hell!"

Under savage fire, the two soldiers sprang to their feet and ran to the water. The screams of the wounded echoed between explosions and shouted orders, but Captain John Westing and Private Ben Moses were oblivious to it all, as they jumped onto the wagon.

"Git on, mules!" Little Ben shouted, while laying the reins to their backs.

John took the carbine off the dead driver and held on as the mules bolted. An explosion drenched the two men and sent a foot soldier flying over their heads, but in seconds the mules were up the bank, and two soldiers and a Gatling gun were headed up San Juan Hill. . . .

A year later, John Westing sat on the balcony of his father's estate near Williamsburg, Virginia, and watched the quivering legs of the baby he held in his arms. "That's all right, Lilly," he said softly. "Your mother's here now."

Elizabeth bent down and took the baby in her arms. "She's just hungry, dear," she said.

John smiled. "I think she prefers a little expertise as opposed to my clumsiness, Elizabeth."

Over in the pines, a mourning dove cooed. John closed his eyes and a smile came to his lips. He opened his eyes and looked over at his wife and child. "It is so peaceful here."

"Yes, it is," Elizabeth replied.

"I thought I might not see it again, Elizabeth." He looked into the eyes of his wife. "I thought I might not have this, with you and the baby."

Elizabeth reached out her hand, and he grasped it firmly. "But you do, John, and I thank God for it every day."

John nodded. "God and Little Ben Moses," he answered. He looked down through the tree-tops at the sparkling river below the bluff and shook his head in disbelief. "Life is a strange thing, Elizabeth," he said slowly.

Elizabeth rocked the baby in her arms and agreed with a nod.

John continued, "Little Ben saved my life, and they decorated *me*." He rubbed his chin thoughtfully, then added, "And all that man came back with was malaria."

"But you gave him something, John, and that is greater than any medal."

"Yes, I hope so."

"It is, John, for as it was once a symbol of my love for you, it is now a symbol of your friendship with Ben."

The door behind them opened then, and a maid approached them. "Cap'n Westing, Miss

Elizabeth, there's someone downstairs to see you."

"Oh, good!" John smiled as he rose from his chair. "Thank you, Mary." He gently took the baby from his wife and gave her to Mary, then took Elizabeth's hand. "Come, Elizabeth, I have waited months for this day."

Elizabeth arose and walked beside her husband, down the long stairway to the foyer. She could sense John's excitement as he reached out his hand to greet a giant of a man, the man who had saved his life. The moment was splendid!

"Elizabeth," her husband announced proudly, "may I introduce to you our new foreman, Benjamin Moses."

Hope

The holidays were bad, but at least they came only a few times during the year. Christmas and Thanksgiving were the hardest of them. But Sundays -- they were the hardest times of all. Sunday was the day they used to sleep a little later than usual. Except Stephen, who would rise before everyone else in the house and go into the kitchen. Flapjacks, eggs and bacon -- that was the breakfast menu on Sunday. Stephen was the chef. By the time June came into the kitchen, he'd have coffee poured and her place by the window prepared.

"Good morning, Juney Bug," he'd tease, with a kiss.

She'd smile and say that he was the best husband a girl could have, and he would agree.

Then they would watch the avenue outside their home come to life. Mr. and Mrs. Brown would pull out of their driveway at seven o'clock sharp in order to be on time for the services at their church, an hour's drive away. The Clarks, who lived in the two-story clapboard house with the wrap-around porch, would walk their dog at about the same time. And at any minute, there would be the plunk of a Sunday newspaper against the front door. On Sunday morning before the children got up, Stephen and June would talk about things they didn't have time to discuss during the week. Stephen loved it back then. He loved to hear the children running along the upstairs hallway and thumping down the stairs.

"Slow down," June would warn them, but they couldn't slow down. Their eagerness to be part of the day wouldn't allow it, but their footsteps would get quieter.

Stephen loved to see their faces in the morning. Smiles and sleepy eyes. Laney, the older child, with her auburn hair and turned-up nose, was such a little tomboy at five years of age. She loved her mother, but adored her father. A kiss and a hug were enough for June, but Stephen would haul his daughter up onto his knee for some serious teasing. "The preacher called and says to leave you home today, Laney girl," he'd say with a serious tone in his voice.

She would frown. "Why?"

"Seems that the little boys in your Sunday school class are having trouble concentrating on the lesson when you're around," he answered, with a concerned look.

Laney would roll her eyes and shake her head. "Quit it, Daddy," she'd say.

Now Travis was a listener. He didn't say much, especially when there was food to be eaten. And at three and a half, he was a real study in the "mind-over-matter" theory. He thought there was absolutely nothing he couldn't do. So Stephen and June were always reminding him of things he would need to remember. Things like "Birds can fly, but people can't."

After church on Sundays, when the weather was fair, Stephen would drive the family out to the country. They'd have a picnic by a trout stream, and sometimes Laney would catch a fish or two. June stayed busy keeping Travis out of the water. Stephen loved it all. He would fish a while with his daughter, then give Travis a ride on his shoulders. The boy would laugh and grab onto tree branches. June said he was part monkey, so he would mimic the chimpanzees he had seen at the traveling shows.

"Watch out, Barnum and Bailey," Stephen teased. "Here's the next *Greatest Show on Earth.*"

June laughed and took her little "monkey" off his dad's shoulders. "Not this boy," she said. "He's gonna be a doctor, or maybe the President."

But it didn't matter to Stephen or his wife what they might someday become. It only mattered that they grow up happy and healthy. That is all any parent should want when their children are small. It's all any prayer should be. The rest is life, and life rules.

Yes, Sundays were good. But that time was gone. It had been almost five years since the last picnic in the country. Stephen still got up early on Sunday mornings, but he wasn't the chef anymore. There were no long, quiet talks with June, or the scuttle of little feet on the upstairs floors. The Browns still left at seven o'clock for their church service, and the Clarks still walked their dog. A lot of things were the same as they had been five years earlier.

But Stephen's life was no longer as it had been. An accident had left him crippled. He walked with a cane. But that wasn't the worst of it. He would have given both of his legs, even his life, if only they had lived. They had not. Stephen was a good driver, but he misjudged the weather, and before he could get over the mountain one Sunday afternoon, a cloud settled in and hindered his vision so that he could not see any distance. Automobiles were new back then. You were much more likely to meet a buckwagon or a horse on the road than a car.

It was a buckwagon with a driver and a passenger that Stephen ran up on that day. They could not have been more than ten paces in front of his car when he finally saw them. He pulled the brake and swerved. There were no railings to keep a car from going off the edge of those narrow mountain roads back then.

Sometimes Stephen would wake up in a cold sweat. He'd seen it all happening again and heard their screams. There would be Laney sitting in the back seat and little Travis in his mother's lap. And when it would happen, he'd always do the same thing, reach over and try to protect them. It was no use. They were all gone before the car even came to rest against those giant hemlocks fifty feet down the mountainside. Only Stephen had stayed in the car, and he was about as mangled as it was. No one knew how he survived in what was left of it. It didn't even look like a car. But he did survive, and for hours he crawled around on that mountainside and collected the bodies of his family. When help came, they found him hunkered down in a crevice between a big rock and a blowdown. They were a hundred feet away from the car, and it was raining. He had June lying close beside him, and he was holding those two children and rocking them just as if they were alive. The rescuers heard him singing. That's how they found him.

"Don't wake them," he pleaded.

They took the children from his bloody arms.

"They're sleeping," he told them. "They're all asleep."

For five years Stephen had tried to put it all in perspective. His and June's families had done and said all they could to help him. His friends had tried. The preacher and the church folks had said and done all they knew how. They tried until they felt helpless. No one likes to feel that way, so after a while, they fell away, one by one. The preacher still talked to Stephen about finding himself again and about how the Lord is always there when you need him, but it didn't stop the dreams, and it did not bring back the family that he had lost.

"For every door that closes, another one opens," the preacher told him.

Stephen would go to bed at night, visualizing a door. He could see the closed one, but he could not seem to find an open one.

His job kept him sane, and he busied himself as much as possible, but the void left by June and the children was too great and always he felt himself slipping more and more into darkness and despair.

Ending it all was something he had thought about for some time. So one Sunday, on a date that coincided with the end of his happiness, he walked slowly up the stairs to the attic. It was mid-morning, and the sun was just coming out of the clouds. Stephen had been awake for hours, going through old pictures and remembering. He had not been in the attic since before the accident, and at the top of the stairs, he saw a little red wooden cart and horse. They stood there as if their owner would soon return. Stephen remembered the children playing in the attic on rainy days. He stooped and picked up the toy and stared at it. He put it down on a cluttered table and walked to a locked cabinet. The sun, shining through the small attic window, lent a golden tone to old clothes and dusty toys as Stephen took a key from his pocket and fitted it to the lock. Behind that door was the end of his life. June had always been afraid of it.

"Lock it up, Stephen," she had pleaded. "We live in a good neighborhood, and the children are so inquisitive."

Stephen had given in to the wish of his wife. The cabinet had not been unlocked in years, but he knew it was there. He had thought about it many times since the accident. There were four bullets in the chamber. He remembered that, too.

He turned the key and thought about what the preacher had said about doors. "When one door closes, another one opens."

Stephen's heart was racing as the lock clicked open. He removed what he had come for and leaned his head against the cabinet door. He pulled a picture from his breast pocket with one hand and looked at it. They were all there. He, June, and the children. He remembered the day it was taken, and the tears began to well in his eyes. The sorrow in his heart was so great that he fell to his knees, sobbing, and the picture dropped from his hand.

"Oh, God, help me!" he cried out from the depths of his heart. His tears fell upon dusty boards until a pool formed at his knees. And when he could weep no more, he lay down and closed his eyes, exhausted.

He imagined a door and for a while, it was closed. Then there was something. A light. Yes, he thought, the door had opened slightly, and there was a light behind it. He strained his mind's eye to see, but he was so weary. Finally he opened his eyes. It was then that Stephen saw something glimmer in a speck of sunlight that touched the dusty floor beside an open trunk. He stared at it for a time before he crawled over to it. He thought, at first, it was a child's toy; then he recognized the object. It had fallen out of its case. It had belonged to June. Stephen took the object into his hand and remembered it had been given to him by a stranger, and he, in turn, had presented it to his wife. A few months before the accident, she had asked him if he had seen it. He had not. Perhaps the children had played with it and dropped it here, he thought. Laney loved her mother's jewelry and mementos.

Stephen stood up and examined the object. A streak of sunlight seemed to bring it to life, and it glistened in the palm of his hand. Its beauty was radiant, and as he traced its shape with his finger, he saw a word inscribed on a clear page. "Love," he read. A calmness came over the man as he remembered the words spoken to him so long ago. "Enjoy its beauty, and understand its meaning, for it is in us all. Then, pass it on."

Stephen suddenly realized that until that moment he had not fulfilled that which was requested of him, for in his youth he had only seen it as a pretty bauble, a gift for his young wife. He could not even remember seeing the word on its page. But now he did, and with it he saw something else.

It was then that the sound of a child crying came to his ears. Stephen placed the object in its wooden case and put it in his pocket. He looked out the window and saw a little girl sitting on the curb in front of his house and weeping.

Without hesitation he ran down the stairs and opened his front door. He walked out of the door and down the walkway to the avenue where the child sat. She was a beautiful girl of about five or six, with long blonde hair and large brown eyes. Tears streaked her round, tanned cheeks, as Stephen knelt beside her.

"Now, what's this, little girl?" he asked, offering her a handkerchief. "Has someone hurt you?"

She took the handkerchief and rubbed her eyes. "I'm lost," she cried. "We just moved here, and I was walking and –" She cried harder.

"Well, don't you worry, now, because I've lived here for a long time, and I know these parts pretty well. I bet I can help you find your house."

The girl looked up at Stephen and swallowed. "You can?" she asked.

"Oh, sure," he told her with a grin. "Just describe it to me and take my hand," he extended his hand. "By the way, what's your name? Mine's Stephen."

The girl sniffled and stood up. "I'm Molly."

"All right then, Molly, let's walk around the block and find something familiar to you."

The girl took the man's hand and soon was on the porch of her new house two streets away. An attractive, yet anxious, woman was overjoyed to see her daughter back home, safe and sound.

"We just moved in, and I'm afraid that Molly got a little bored while I was arranging our furniture. Thank you for bringing her home." The woman's voice was pleasant, and she seemed genuine.

"I was glad to help, Mrs. –"

"Oh, I'm sorry." She seemed flustered. "My name is Jenny. Jenny Lewis. Molly and I moved here from Fredricksburg. I'm a school teacher."

She extended her hand, and Stephen reciprocated.

"I'm Stephen Bartley," he responded. "It's so nice to meet you both. Welcome to town."

Molly smiled. "I like him, Mama. He's nice. Can he come in?"

Stephen smiled back, his face somewhat flushed.

The girl's mother looked at her daughter, then back at the man. He was polite and handsome, and she felt comfortable in his presence. She urged her daughter into the house, and Stephen turned to leave.

"Mr. Bartley," she called. "I hope you do not think it forward of me, but so that you will better understand my daughter's question, I should tell you that my husband, her father, passed away a year ago. She misses him terribly, and I, well, I think she, well, uh –"

Stephen waved his hand and said, "I understand, Mrs. Lewis. I, too, lost my wife and children some time ago."

"I'm sorry," offered the woman with a pained expression on her face.

Stephen nodded. "It was an accident."

Jenny Lewis reached into her dress pockets for a moment and fidgeted a bit.

Stephen stood there quietly, feeling a little awkward, but just as he was thinking he should leave, he found himself wishing he could stay and come to know Jenny Lewis and her daughter better.

"Mr. Bartley, I know we're practically strangers, but if you would like to come in for lunch, we would love to have you."

"I would like that very much, Mrs. Lewis," he smiled.

Just inside the front door, a little girl crinkled her nose and quietly clapped her hands. "Yes!" she whispered.

A new door had definitely opened, not for one person, but for three people. When Stephen Bartley did pass on the crystal rose soon after he and Jenny Lewis were married, he retained forever a lesson he had learned: Where there is love, there is always hope.

The Gift

The young girl peered around the bedroom door and quietly entered the room. "Mama," she said softly, "are you awake?"

The woman lying on the bed turned her face towards her daughter. A weak smile formed on her lips, and she answered, "I'm awake, dear. I was just looking at the birds there at the feeder." She turned her head back towards the window. A wooden platform was base for a glass receptacle which released tiny seeds for the hungry feathered creatures just as an hourglass releases sand.

Nell walked around the foot of the bed and sat on its edge.

"Look at them," her mother chuckled. "They must be starving, poor things!"

Nell looked out the window, as a bright red cardinal took his place among the greedy beaks, forcing two wrens off the platform. They flitted over to the clothesline and then down into the yard where they hopped about in their eager search for anything edible.

The screen door at the rear of the house slammed, and the wrens flushed into the air.

"Nell, where are you?" a voice called.

Nell looked down at her mother and squeezed her damp hand. "It's Billy," she said. "I'll be back in a minute with lunch."

With that, the girl was up and turning the corner of the bed, when her mother said, "Nell, make sure he washes his hands before he eats."

"I will," responded the girl as she slipped through the doorway.

The woman took a deep breath and turned her face again towards the window and the birds.

"I won you somethin', Nell," said the boy, as he unscrewed the lid of the pickle jar.

His sister walked by him as if his words did not concern her in the least. She reached in front of him and removed the jar lid from his dirty hands and screwed it back on the barrel-like jar. "Go wash your hands, Billy, or you're going to get the biggest parasite in your stomach that you could ever imagine." Nell reached up and opened a cabinet door. She placed the pickle jar on a shelf and closed the door.

Billy looked at his dirty fingers, then popped the remaining pickle into his mouth and reached for the spigot.

"Uh, uh," warned his sister. "Not in the kitchen, boy. You know better than that."

Billy shrugged and trudged off to the bathroom, muttering.

Nell finished preparing his sandwich and sliced an apple before her brother returned. She placed them on a plate and set it on the table beside a tall, cool glass of milk.

Billy saluted her upon his return and held out his hands for her inspection.

Nell smiled and sat down. "Eat your lunch, Billy," she said.

"Thanks, Sis." The boy bit into his sandwich.

Nell nodded and turned the page of a catalog.

"What you looking for, Nell?"

"Don't talk with your mouth full," cautioned the girl.

Billy gulped a swallow of milk. He looked curiously at the catalog, which was upside down to him.

Nell closed it and replied flatly, "Nothing."

"Well, if I was looking for nothin', I sure wouldn't look in a Sears Roebuck Catalog, Sis," he offered with a grin, "'cause it's just full of something on near 'bout every page." He took another big bite of his sandwich and smiled.

"It'll be Mother's Day on Sunday, Billy." Nell pushed away from the table and stood up. "I was just looking."

Billy stopped chewing and lost his smile.

Nell removed a pitcher from the icebox and poured lemonade into a glass with a yellow and orange flower painted on it. She stood at the sink and looked out of the kitchen window. Outside, the sun shone brightly. Robins searched the freshly cut lawn for worms, and out under the shade tree a gentle breeze moved the swing back and forth. Jenny Sue, the cat, came across the yard to her food dish beside the back door, and robins flew to the safety of leafy branches.

Quietly, Billy rose from his chair and placed his empty plate and glass on the counter next to the sink. Nell didn't notice until the boy touched her arm. "Nell," he said, almost in a whisper.

She looked at him with sad eyes.

"I won you somethin'!" he said, as he

reached down deep into his pants pocket. He brought out a bracelet with dangling moons and stars on it and fastened it around his sister's small wrist. "It ain't much, Sis," he admitted. "That ain't real gold or nothin', but it sure is pretty."

Nell held her wrist up to the window and smiled. "It sure is, Billy," she agreed. "Thank you."

The boy looked down at the glass of lemonade. "Well, you do a lot for us, Nell. And I just kinda wanted to--"

"I know, Billy," the girl interrupted. She pulled her younger brother to her and tousled his hair. "Now, you'd better go give Mama this lemonade and a kiss and then get back to the store, or Daddy's going to get you good."

She watched as the boy walked out of the kitchen and down the hall towards their mother's room. A few minutes later, he was out the back door and across the yard.

"Don't y'all be late, Billy," she called. "Or supper will be cold."

The boy waved back at his sister and hurried along the sidewalk.

Jenny Sue meowed at the screen door, and Nell opened it and let her in. She reached down and picked up the white Persian. "Look, Jenny

Sue," she said, holding out her wrist. She shook the bracelet, and the cat pawed at the dangling trinkets. "You can't have it, girl," she laughed. "Billy gave it to me."

Later that day, Nell sat in a chair beside her mother's bed and read to her from the newspaper. This was something she did every day. Not because her mother couldn't read, but because Nell loved to read. In school she had been one of the best readers in her class. But that was before her mother became so very ill, before her weak heart had finally incapacitated her. When she could no longer walk from her bedroom to the kitchen without the aid of her husband or one of the children, something had to be done. It had been decided that Nell would stay at home with her mother and take on the responsibilities required. School was second to this, and, besides, there was no one else.

The store which her father, Walker Jenkins, owned and operated was a full-time venture; and although he and the boys, Billy and older brother Ned, could check in at home from time to time during the day, someone had to be there constantly. The house had to be kept, meals had to be prepared, and Rachael Jenkins had to be cared for.

The poor woman, who was only in her late

thirties, could hardly leave the bed, let alone tend to the least physical chore. She had been bedridden for almost a year. Nell had taken on the household and nursing responsibilities as few could. She was only thirteen and yet her parents and even her brothers marveled at how well she dealt with the situation. Never was the house in a shambles, or a meal unprepared. And, always, the child did all she could to make her mother as comfortable as possible. She bathed her daily and changed the linens on her bed so that they were always fresh and clean. She made sure that the draperies were open every morning so that the small room where her mother spent most of her time was kept bright. And, once a day in suitable weather, she would help her mother into a wheelchair and roll her out on the front porch where the sun could touch her pale skin while they talked. It had been Nell's idea for the bird feeder to be placed outside her mother's window. Billy made sure it was always filled with seed.

Rachael Jenkins watched her daughter as the girl read to her. In her heart was a mixture of pride and guilt. How beautiful she is, thought Rachael, as Nell sat there reading aloud to her as if there was nothing else she would rather do. Nell was a gift from God, and her mother knew it. Never did she complain, and always she was there to lend a cheerful smile or word during her mother's difficult times.

But there were times when Rachael Jenkins wondered about her daughter, times when the girl would read her to sleep and then she'd awaken and watch the profile of her daughter's face as she stared out the window. It couldn't be easy, Rachael knew, to give up one's girlhood.

"Nell," the woman said, stopping her daughter from reading.

The girl lowered the paper and looked at her mother. "Yes, Mama?"

Rachael motioned for her to put the paper to one side and then reached out and held her daughter's hand. "You know the cruise I've always wanted to take? Remember the ships we looked at in the magazines when you were a little girl?"

Nell smiled and nodded her head, "Yes, I remember."

Her mother took a deep breath and spoke. "Well, your father and the boys have been putting some money away for a while and have saved up enough for Walker and me to sail to Boston from Newport News. Look," she said, as she opened a pamphlet that had been lying on her nightstand. "It's the *Princess Bartania*. Isn't it luxurious?"

Nell looked at the picture, while her mother continued talking. "We'll take the train to Newport News and board the ship there on the seventeenth. We arrive in Boston on the twenty-first, and check into the hospital then. It works out perfectly." The woman was excited. "Walker says it's a Mother's Day present from you all."

Nell smiled. She had been told about the cruise by her father.

"It is something she has always wanted, Nell," he had told her. "I don't know how things in Boston are going to go. She's so weak now. Perhaps the cruise will lift her spirits and give her strength, so that they can perform the operation." Walker Jenkins was a strong man, but his voice was filled with emotion that night as he told his daughter of his intentions. Nell could not help thinking that, in his heart, her father saw the cruise as a last gift to the woman he loved.

So on the outside that day, as her mother spoke to her, the girl smiled. But, inside, her heart wept.

Two days later Nell stood at the bureau in her room and slipped on her best dress. It was pale blue, and she wore it over a white, long-sleeved blouse with a rounded collar. Her mother especially liked it, and Billy and Ned always told her she looked real pretty in that outfit. She wasn't so sure of how pretty she was, but the clothes were fine for a walk down town.

The girl brushed her long, brown hair and frowned at the natural curls that she could do nothing about. Finally, she pulled it back and pinned it in a bun. "There," she said.

"Nell," called her older brother from the kitchen table. "You ready?"

Ned was off from the store for half a day and had told his sister that he'd stay with their mother while the girl went to town. He was preparing toast and juice when Nell walked into the room.

"You look great, Nell," he said.

Nell shrugged and poured herself some juice in a glass. She drank it and turned to her brother. "She likes to talk for a while after breakfast. Then she'll take a nap for an hour." The girl washed out her glass and placed it on the drying rack next to the sink. "I'll be home by lunch time so you can get on back to the store."

Ned walked over to his sister and, placing his hand on her shoulder, gently turned her towards him. "The cruise is really from all of us, Nell. It's not just about the money. What you do around here is priceless, and we all know it." Ned looked at the tears in his sister's eyes, and he offered her his handkerchief. She took it, and he hugged her tight. "Mama knows it, too, girl. Better than anyone."

Nell wiped her eyes. "I just want to give her a little something, Ned. Something just from me."

"I know, Sis." Ned picked up the plate of toast and the glass of juice for his mother and walked out of the kitchen.

Nell took her purse from the kitchen table and opened the screen door. Jenny Sue, the cat, rushed by her ankle as she stepped out of the house. "Stay off the draperies, Jenny," she called back.

It was a perfect spring day, and the walk to town was pleasant. Nell turned down a couple of offers for rides, preferring rather to enjoy the morning sunshine and the songbirds that flitted about the branches of oaks and maples that lined the road on both sides and formed a shady canopy. Squirrels chased each other playfully and chattered from leaf-filled crevices.

"Good morning, Nell." Nell saw old Mrs. Putnam sweeping off her front porch.

The girl paused and replied, "Good morning, Mrs. Putnam."

"How's your mother doing?" The woman leaned on her broomstick and wiped the dampness from her chin.

"She's doing all right, ma'am. Going up to Boston next week, you know."

"We'll be praying for her. You tell her that, now."

Nell smiled. "I will. See you later."

"Bye, Nell," answered the woman.

Nell walked onto Main Street a few minutes later and headed straight for the jewelry store. She had been thinking that a brooch, or perhaps a necklace, might be on sale, and she was anxious to see what they had on display.

When she stepped into the jewelry shop, she noticed there were only two customers browsing along the shelves at the rear of the store. Immediately, a pleasant middle-aged lady approached her. "Could I help you, young lady?" she asked.

"Where are your pendants?" the girl responded.

The lady smiled and guided her back to an area where pendants and brooches were encased in glass. "Anything in particular?" The lady moved around to the opposite side of the glass enclosure.

Nell looked at the beautiful pieces of jewelry. "No, ma'am," she answered. "Nothing in particular. I'll know it when I see it." But Nell had already seen something that dashed her hopes.

The prices, though not exorbitant, were more than she could afford. The girl's heart sank.

"Excuse me," a customer called from the rear of the shop.

The clerk smiled at Nell. "I'll be right back," she said, as she walked away.

Nell moved to a sale display, but nothing there caught her eye. Nothing that spoke to her to buy it. What she wanted was something special, but she had too little money in her purse to purchase anything more than mediocre.

As she walked out of the jewelry store, she felt a lump in her throat. Where else could she go, she wondered. For two weeks she had thought she might be able to afford something beautiful, but now she knew that it was not possible.

She crossed the street and sat on a bench in the shade beneath an elm tree in front of the courthouse. She watched as people walked by on the sidewalk. A girl who looked to be about her age walked alongside her mother. They had just come out of the corner drug store and were laughing about something and talking. Nell watched them pass by. She didn't know the girl, but she envied her. She had never walked down Main Street with her own mother. There were so many things that she had missed. No, she thought. You mustn't think like that. You simply do what you must do. You don't question, and you never envy. It's just not right.

Nell bit the inside of her lip. There I go, she thought, feeling sorry for myself. Be thankful for what you have, she told herself. Count your blessings.

Nell closed her eyes and said a prayer. It was short, but it was from her heart. And those are the ones that are heard. "Heartfelt and selfless words drift to heaven on the wings of angels." Her mother had told her that when Nell was a little girl.

"Hello." The man's voice was soft and deep.

Nell opened her eyes and was surprised that the elderly gentleman had sat down on the bench next to her without her even knowing it. At first she was startled, but there was something about him that soon set her at ease.

"Hello," she answered.

The gentleman crossed his leg over a knee and turned slightly towards the girl. His face was handsome, yet creased with age, and his eyes were vivid blue. They captured her attention. "My name is Matthew, young lady," he said. "I'm sorry to have startled you."

"Oh, it's all right. I was just, well, uh –" Nell was flustered.

The gentleman smiled. "Waiting for the day to unfold, I'm sure," he offered.

Nell smiled and nodded her head. She told the gentleman her name.

Matthew put out his hand, and Nell shook it. "Well, Nell, my train leaves for Roanoke in an hour, and I was just walking about your town and enjoying its peacefulness."

"Yes," agreed the girl. "It is quiet here."

"Have you lived here all your life?"

"Yes. All my life. My father owns a store just west of the town limits. I have two brothers."

"Older?"

"Well, Ned is older. He graduated from school last year and works with Daddy. Billy is younger. He goes to school and helps out at the store."

Matthew nodded. "And, you, Nell. What do you do?"

Nell looked across the street and then back at the old gentleman. The thought occurred to her that she could get up and leave, or just shake her head and not answer him. But something inside her wanted to speak. And, strangely enough, she trusted this man. He was gentle and seemed genuinely interested. Besides, in an hour he would be gone and with him all that she might say. "Well," she began, "I went to school until last year when I had to stop to be at home with my mother."

"Is she ill?" asked the man.

"Yes. Her heart is very weak, and she can hardly get around. But there's this doctor in Boston who can do an operation that could make her better."

"Is she going for the operation?"

"Oh, yes," replied the girl. "Next week."

The old gentleman nodded his head. "I hope it all works out, Nell," he said in a concerned voice.

"Thank you." Nell became quiet.

Matthew broke the silence. "You cook and clean and take care of everyone?"

"Yes."

"That's a lot of weight on your shoulders, Nell," remarked Matthew.

"I don't mind, Mr., uh –" Nell looked at the man in anticipation.

He smiled. "Matthew. Just call me Matthew."

"I don't really mind, Matthew," she continued. "I mean, we are able to talk a lot, and I enjoy reading to her, and the chores are not so bad because Daddy and the boys help me out. They're not messy at all."

"What about friends?"

"Well, there's not much time for that, but on Sunday I see Katie Bingham and Angela Rainey at church. We sit together. They were in my class in school. And they tell me what's going on with everybody."

"Do you miss school?"

Nell shrugged her shoulders slightly. "Yes, I miss it. I was a good student. But I read Billy's school books, and I'm real good with numbers."

Matthew smiled. "Sounds to me like you're quite a girl, Nell."

"I don't know about that, Matthew. Sometimes I wish it was different, you know. I see other girls and their mothers and think about what it would be like. But you do what you have to do 'cause it doesn't do any good to wish for something that can't be. So I just pray."

"What do you pray for, Nell?"

Nell found a fluffy white cloud in the sky and followed it with her eyes, thinking. "I pray that Mama won't suffer. And that my daddy and brothers will be strong, and that I can do all I need to do. That's really all, I guess."

Matthew looked at the girl sitting next to him, and he was moved by her humility, her honesty, and her devotion.

"What do you want, Nell?" he asked quietly.

"I want –" she began, then paused and continued, "I want to give my Mama a wonderful gift to take with her to Boston, but –"

Matthew interrupted, "But you can't afford such a gift?"

Nell sighed. "Matthew, I don't have very much money, and all the pretty things cost so much."

Matthew looked into the girl's eyes. "Oh, Nell," he said, while reaching into his coat pocket. "I am an old man. Perhaps that is why I can tell you that you possess something far greater than money and much more wonderful than anything it can purchase. Let me show you."

The man opened a small wooden box and took out the most beautiful object Nell had ever seen. "Look closely, Nell," he said. "The answer is there, on the page next to the rose."

Nell examined the exquisite crystal rose and touched its emerald leaves with her small fingers. And then she saw the word on the page it lay across. Her eyes filled with tears as she looked up into Matthew's face. "Love," she said in a whisper.

The old gentlemen smiled and nodded. "This you have given, Nell. There is no greater gift."

At that moment, Nell Jenkins' guilt, as

imagined as it might have been, was washed away, and she knew beyond any doubt that the man who sat next to her on the courtyard bench was right.

Matthew closed the box and handed it to the girl. He lifted the watch from his vest pocket and saw the time. "I've got a train to catch," he said, while rising to his feet.

Nell stood up, also, and offered him the box. "I couldn't!" she protested.

The man smiled. "That's what I said. But it was given to me anyway. There is something about it that enables you to see beyond your doubts. It brings light to the shadows, Nell. Give it to your mother."

The man bowed slightly and reached out his hand.

Nell put her hand in his.

"It was nice to meet you, Nell. I wish you a long and good life."

"Thank you, Matthew," replied the girl. She watched the old gentleman leave, then put the wooden box in her purse and started home. . .

A few days later, Walker and Rachael Jenkins bid tearful farewells to their children and boarded the *Princess Bartania* at Newport News. Their cruise was marked by fair weather, and each day they lounged on sunny decks and marveled at the greatness of the ocean. They reminisced and touched again upon those things that had drawn them together. Walker Jenkins thought it was good to hear the laughter of his wife again, and for those few days aboard ship, he was a happy man. He knew he had at least fulfilled one of her dreams.

When they arrived in port, Walker summoned a taxi, and the couple was transferred to Boston Hospital, where later Dr. John Lieberman would examine Rachael. When, after many tests had been conducted in the following days and several conferences called, the doctor met Walker in his office, Walker knew that the prognosis was not going to be good.

Since their arrival Walker Jenkins had watched his wife's condition deteriorate. His hopes that the cruise would somehow strengthen her were dashed, for although her spirit had improved, her diseased heart had not.

"She is too weak," the doctor told him. "And even to begin the surgery would be too much stress on her heart. The odds are too great that she would not survive."

So Walker Jenkins stayed with his wife and was strong every minute from dawn until dusk. Late at night when she slept, he would leave her and walk across the street to his hotel room, alone and afraid.

It was on the fifth morning after their arrival that Walker found his wife sitting up in bed, folding the last of four letters she had written.

She smiled and greeted him with a kiss. Then she laid the letters aside and motioned for her husband to come and sit beside her.

He pulled open the window draperies and took her hands in his. He squeezed them and felt her weakness.

A smile came across her face, and for a moment her eyes sparkled in the morning sunlight.

"I'll get your breakfast, dear," Walker spoke quietly, hopefully.

Rachael shook her head. "No, Walker, I'm not hungry." She licked her lips and swallowed. "I want you to know that I loved the cruise."

Walker smiled with trembling lips and kissed her frail hands as he listened.

"And I want you to know that I love you with all my heart. I am only sorry that I could not be stronger. It would have been such a gift to grow old with you and to watch our children become adults. There seems an unfairness in this, but I have been so blessed."

Walker fought back his tears. "I don't want

you to go, Rachael. I can't see me without you." Tears began to trickle down the man's face, falling onto the gown of his wife.

Rachael cupped his face in her hands. "I will always be in your heart, my husband, forever young, forever your wife." She kissed him and turned her head towards the window and the bed table, where lay an open wooden box and the crystal rose. Her face brightened, and she smiled. "Look," she said.

Walker raised his eyes and saw that the morning sunlight had cast its beams onto the rose, sending prisms of color against the walls and bedsheets. The effect was awesome, yet ever so delicate. He smiled through his tears. "It is so beautiful," he said.

But his wife did not hear. Only her spirit, as it became adrift in the colors of love. . . .

A month after the funeral of Rachael Jenkins, Nell gently unfolded the letter her mother had written to her and read it in silence:

My Dearest Nell,

How does a mother say all that is in her heart when there is so little time? We missed so much because of my illness -- so much that I wish we could have experienced together. I am sorry for that. And I am sorry for the times in your future when I will not be there to hold you and to reassure you of your strength. I can only pray that you will remember me in the little things, and the quiet times. Things that I have said -- like "I love you" or "You are beautiful" or "I am proud of you." Times when I tucked you into bed at night, or told you a story of my childhood that made you giggle, or even when I consoled your broken heart. I can only hope that I have given you enough of my love to last your lifetime.

As for you, I could not have been blessed with a more wonderful daughter. You have been my shining star amid the darkness. You are the hope of my prayers and the pride of my heart. Thank you for all that you have done.

Be happy, my darling, and remember me in your heart throughout your life. I know we will see each other again someday, and then we will walk together.

Until that time, I will watch you from afar and speak to you in whispers.

Love you, forever,
Mama

P.S.

I love the crystal rose you gave me. It is so beautiful. I keep it on my bed table and look at it often. It brings me such comfort.

Yesterday I was feeling somewhat sorry for myself, and then I saw the beauty of the rose and read *that one little word that someone inscribed on the page of that little book. It made me think that, for all the love I have given, I have received so much more. It really is the only thing we bring here, and the only thing that we can take when we leave. Love, always.*

Mother Love

Samuel Lively walked briskly beneath a darkening afternoon sky. Rain seemed imminent; yet he somehow knew it would not come. No one had told him that. He just felt it, and that was good enough for him.

"Hello, Mr. Lively," smiled a woman he passed on the sidewalk.

"Hello," he responded politely. Beneath his breath he murmured "160." He turned the corner and continued his counting. He always counted his steps around town. And he remembered the numbers, too. There were 973 steps from his front door to the threshold of his office on East Third

Street, across from Hanby's Bakery. If he crossed Third Street and walked to the end of the counter where Mr. Hanby displayed his fresh-baked cinnamon swirls every morning, that one-way stroll added a total of thirty-one steps. Hurrying, however, would lessen the paces needed to between twenty-five and twenty-eight.

There was a low rumble in the sky. Samuel did not look up, but kept looking ahead to where a moderate crowd was gathering in the front yard of a well-known house on Blount Street which had recently lost its owner, a kind yet extremely private woman. "Miss Lilly," folks called her. Her real name was Lillian W. Vanderling, whose husband had died some thirty years ago.

The Vanderling name adorned a plaque beneath a stained glass window in the Presbyterian Church over on Locust Street. In their day the Vanderlings had been on the guest list of every party host or hostess in town. They also entertained in their spacious home, and many were the guests who enjoyed their hospitality.

But after David Vanderling's death, the house on Blount Street became still and lifeless. No more did its rooms echo with laughter and the tinkling of fine crystal. No more did it shine brighter than any other house in town, for seldom was there more than dim lamplight to be seen by an inquisitive passerby. Lillian Vanderling lived alone for a few years until one day when she was visited by a stranger.

Samuel Lively had known the widow of David Vanderling since childhood. He had known her well. . . .

When Samuel was about eight years old, he found himself alone in the world. His father was unknown to him, and his mother, whom he adored, passed slowly from his life with a rare disease in her blood.

An aunt in a distant city could have taken the boy, except that she was selfish and had no use for a rather awkward child with a peculiar sense of order and an interest in numbers which she thought bordered on the absurd. "Why a boy would fill a thimble with sand and then dedicate an hour each evening to separating and counting the granules is beyond me!" she had stated to the lawyer in the cramped and darkened living room of the house soon after his mother had died. When the woman noticed Samuel standing in the doorway, she blushed and touched her damp chin with a scented handkerchief, then mumbled a few words to the lawyer. Samuel knew she didn't want him, so when she forced a smile and kissed and patted his forehead, he closed his eyes and turned away. She paused for a moment, then stepped heavily through the hallway and out the front door. The lawyer escorted her to her car. The boy counted her footsteps as she left.

Samuel went into the small bedroom where his mother had spent the last days and nights of her life. He did not want to forget one thing about her. There was not much there in the way of furnishings. A washstand in a far corner, a table and mirror where he would watch her "put on her face" in the morning. Next to the closet door there was a bookshelf that was not by any means full of books. It held a few of the classics and an assortment of children's stories. Samuel looked at the titles. He knew them well, for he had read them all again and again. The boy ran his fingers along the smooth edge of the shelf until he came to a narrow wooden box between a Bible and a book of poems. He lifted the box from the shelf and stared at it.

The morning sun shone through the only window in the room, casting its light on a rough wooden chair beside his mother's bed. Samuel held the box in his hand and walked over to the chair. He sat down and touched his mother's pillow. "Read me a story," she would say. Samuel laid his head on the pillow. He could smell her fragrance. Remembering her smile as he would read, he closed his eyes and wept silent tears. His heart was broken. "Take the rose, Samuel," she had told him one night. "It was given to me by a stranger."

"Why would a person you did not even know give you such a beautiful gift, Mother?" he had asked.

"I don't know, Son," his mother replied. "That has always been the beauty of it. That only the giver knew the reason." She smiled and touched the petals of the little rose with her fingers. "See the word inscribed on the page?" she asked.

"Yes," answered the boy, as he made out the letters, "L-o-v-e." He saw the tears in his mother's eyes as she spoke in a whisper.

"Remember that, my beautiful boy. It is the only thing we really have. To love and to be loved. Don't ever forget that, Samuel." She put the crystal rose in the boy's small hand and pulled him to her. "Don't let what has happened to me sadden your life. There is so much love in the world. And someone will love you as I have. I promise you that. If only you will open your heart."

Samuel lifted the rose from its box. The morning sunlight played with its colors. He turned it so that he could see the word. "I love you, Mother," he whispered.

The closing of the front door brought Samuel to his feet. He put the rose back in its box and tucked it into his coat pocket. He walked over to the bookshelf and removed the Bible, several other books, and a small picture of his mother as a child and placed them neatly in his suitcase at the foot of the bed.

"Come along, Samuel," called the lawyer, as he picked up his briefcase. "We will see if Mrs. Lindstrom will take you in for a spell." The tall man put his hand on the boy's shoulder and guided him out of the house.

Adelle Lindstrom was known as a kind woman who provided temporary housing to families or individuals in need. Her house, located at the corner of Blount and Early Streets, was quite large, with two spectacular stone chimneys. Samuel knew that the chimney on the east end of the Lindstrom house contained exactly 1,223 outer stones, for he had stood and counted them twice in one day. He wasn't so sure how many the western chimney contained, as it was partially taken over by thick ivy. There, he had been able to count only 1,128 stones.

As he followed the lawyer down the sidewalk, he fell into rhythm with the tall man's steps and would have begun to count them, too, had it not been for a most beautiful butterfly which lit upon the back of the lawyer's dark coat and distracted the boy's attention. He studied it as he walked along. Its wings were black with white stripes, and its tails were long and narrow, with a bright red marking at their base. Samuel reached out his hand to seize the butterfly, but it fluttered into the air above his head and started a zigzag and up-and-down route across the street.

Samuel followed, jumping and grabbing. His attempts to grasp the butterfly were fruitless, and the boy laughed aloud. The lawyer turned and called to him, but Samuel was into his task and did not even hear his name being called. Instead, he followed the beautiful butterfly across the street and up the sidewalk along a low brick wall. The butterfly changed its course, and the boy, too, turned off the sidewalk and up a flight of brick steps. He ran along a brick walkway until the butterfly again turned sharply and fluttered across the yard and around the corner of a house.

Samuel still followed, but when he rounded the corner, he stopped in amazement. He blinked his eyes and shook his head in disbelief. There before him was a cobblestone path bordered by flowering shrubs and trees with smooth intertwining limbs. The fragrance of flowers permeated the air, and Samuel saw that beyond the shrubs were circles and squares and rows of every kind of flower he had ever seen. And many others strange to him. Bright yellow and orange and white daylilies reached up from green and shadowed fingers and tilted towards the morning sun. Pink phlox encircled a moss-covered cement birdbath and swayed with the weight of bees and other winged insects. There were roses and pansies, impatiens and caladiums tucked carefully within stone-bordered islands. Lotus vine and scented geraniums snuggled at the shoulders and crossed legs of a white stone angel with a chipped toe and a cracked wing.

Samuel saw movement in the grass between two flower islands. It was a robin. The orange-breasted bird paid no attention to the boy.

Instead, it studied the ground and cocked its head to the side as if listening for something. In a moment, with a swift movement and a tug at the earth, it brought up a squirming worm in its beak and then flew into a golden chain tree which showered the cobblestone path with color. The sounds of high-pitched chirps came from a shadowed crotch in the tree, before the robin flew down again, its wings fanning the dew from bearded irises.

The drone of bees and the flutter of butter-flies were all around the boy. It was as if he had stepped into an enchanted place, for a profusion of color and beauty and fragrance surrounded him.

Samuel looked at the great red-brick house beside him. He knew this house from the front, but only from a distance. He had never entered its grounds or stood on the steps to its entrance. Instead, he had sat along the brick wall out at the sidewalk on warm days and looked beyond its ivy-laden iron fence into the front yard of the place. He remembered a man and a woman and the sound of laughter. Once he had seen them walking hand in hand. The sight had made him sad, for he longed for a man in his own life, a father, a husband for his mother. On occasion, he had seen the great house all lit up, with fine cars parked in its driveway and out in front.

Now the house was silent except for the sounds of nature around it.

A butterfly darted past the boy and flut-tered erratically along the walkway towards the rear of the house. Samuel stepped forward, then looked behind him and backed up three steps to the corner of the front of the building. He count-ed five cobblestones for the width of the walk-way and then began to walk slowly forward again, counting the outside bricks as he went. The creeping thyme which grew between the bricks and stones threatened to conceal the walkway in some areas, and the boy paused to be sure that no stone was out of place. He made his way slowly and silently until he came to the rear corner of the house. It was then that he heard the sound of a woman weeping.

She cried softly, her back towards the boy, her face in her hands.

Instinctively, Samuel turned to leave, but as he did so, a strange thing occurred. A gentle and fragrant breeze came out of the garden and, with it, a whisper.

Samuel stopped and listened. There were only the sounds of nature. He took another step, and the whisper returned. It was in the wind, yet somehow apart from it. The boy looked back at the woman. Perhaps she had noticed him and called to him gently. But she had not, and still she wept.

For a moment the boy was frightened. He began to step hurriedly away from the woman. Before he had taken a half-dozen steps, the whisper returned. Samuel put his hands over his ears and bowed his head. He stepped to his right and leaned against the warm brick wall of the house. There was no mistake now, for the whisper was audible, even above the rapid pounding of the boy's heart. It said, "The rose."

Samuel removed his hands from his ears and reached into his pocket. He withdrew the small wooden box, then turned and walked back to where the woman sat crying. As he approached her, she turned her head slightly and noticed him. A bit startled, she straightened up and wiped the tears from her eyes.

Samuel spoke first. "I didn't mean to scare you, ma'am," he apologized.

The woman's expression softened. "I thought I was alone," she responded. "Who are you?"

"My name is Samuel," answered the boy.

The woman raised her eyebrows and waited a moment for the last name to come. When it didn't, she smiled and said, "All right, Samuel. Can I help you?"

The boy blushed. "Oh, no! I – I was just chasing a butterfly and followed it here."

The woman looked beyond the boy at the flowers. "Well, did you have any luck finding it?"

"No, ma'am," he answered, "but you sure have a beautiful garden."

"Thank you, young man. I'm afraid I am not such a good gardener. My husband was the gardener. It was his passion."

"I like flowers, too," offered the boy. "But I never had more than a few to take care of."

The woman nodded thoughtfully. She noticed his eyes, how bright and alert they were. His manner was polite and timid. There was something about him that set her at ease, and she motioned him to sit. "Come and sit down, Samuel. It has been a while since I entertained a visitor."

Samuel looked around at the front corner of the house as if he was expecting someone to appear. "Oh, I can't right now, ma'am," he answered. "I was on my way down the street to Mrs. Lindstrom's place, and--"

"Adelle Lindstrom?" questioned the woman.

Samuel nodded his head. "Yes, ma'am. My mother died, and Mr. Henly thinks she might take me in until he can think of what to do about me."

Lilly Vanderling put her hand to her mouth and with sorrowful eyes looked at the young boy. "I'm so sorry about your mother, Samuel."

The boy looked down at his feet, then over at the flowers.

Lilly watched him intently. "Is there any-one in your family that you can live with?"

"Well," replied the boy, "my mother's sister came down for the funeral, but she has all she can handle and doesn't need me to add to it all." He didn't look at the woman, and she knew he was hurt and probably making an excuse.

Lilly couldn't believe that the boy's own aunt would not take him in, regardless of her situation. She herself had never had children, but had always longed for the love of a child. Her heart was full of emotion, when a voice called from around the front of the house.

"Samuel!" It was Mr. Henly. "Samuel, where are you?" he called, from the front of the house. Samuel looked at the woman who was now standing in front of him. Her dark hair and features reminded him of his mother. There was a gentleness in her nature that appealed to the need in his heart, a need for the affection of the mother he had lost. But there was also a sadness in her eyes, a sadness beyond words. "It's Mr. Henly," he said softly. "I have to go now." Samuel reached out and offered the woman his small wooden box. It was not very long, perhaps two and a half inches. It was obvious to Lilly Vanderling that there was some age to it.

She took the box with questioning eyes and was about to speak when the boy said, "It's a gift. A very special gift, and I want you to have it."

"But I --" the woman began.

"Please," the boy interrupted. "Maybe I can come and help you with your flowers sometimes." He turned to leave.

Lilly Vanderling smiled. "I'd like that, Samuel," she said.

The boy smiled back.

"Lillian," came a man's voice.

Lilly looked past Samuel and greeted the lawyer she had known for years. "Hello, George," she replied.

George Henly seemed a bit agitated as he shook his head and apologized for encroaching on her privacy. "Lillian, I'm sorry. The boy got away from me, and--"

The woman interrupted, "No, George. Samuel has been no trouble at all. We were just talking about my flower garden and how the butterflies have taken it over today."

George Henly relaxed his shoulders and looked at the flowers which lined the walkway around the house. "My goodness, Lillian," he marveled. "There must be a thousand daylilies back here!"

The woman crossed her arms and smiled. "David loved those flowers and said he could never plant enough of them."

Samuel saw the happiness in her face when she spoke, but detected a sadness in her voice.

"There are 348," he said.

Lillian looked at the boy in surprise. "What, Samuel?" she asked.

Samuel pointed at the lilies along the cobblestone path. "There are 348 lilies along the path, there," he said. "And another 200 out there in the circle around the birdbath."

"You've counted them?" questioned the astonished woman.

Samuel grinned shyly. "Yes, ma'am," he answered. "They are real pretty and I counted them before I saw you."

Lillian Vanderling looked questioningly at the lawyer.

"The boy counts everything he sees, Lilly," offered the man. He shook his head and shrugged. "I've never seen anything like it."

Lillian looked back at the boy. "What else have you counted, Samuel?"

"Well," responded the boy, "there are exactly six hundred cobblestones in your walkway from the front corner of the house to where your patio begins." Samuel walked to the center of the patio and drew an imaginary circle in the air around him with his hand. "There are another twelve hundred stones here in the patio," he added. "There would have been six more used for the center here," he patted his foot on the rough-faced slate that had been cut into a circle and placed at the center of the patio, "if this piece of slate wasn't put here instead."

"That is amazing, Samuel," exclaimed the woman. The boy grinned and kicked at a cobblestone with his scuffed shoe.

"How did you become so accomplished at calculations, Samuel?" asked Lillian.

Samuel put his forefinger to his chin and contorted his face as if he were contemplating a problem. He looked first at the woman in front of him, then over at George Henly. The lawyer was fidgety. Samuel shrugged his shoulders and answered, "I don't know. I guess I just like numbers."

Lillian smiled. "I should say so."

George Henly glanced at his pocket watch and clicked its glass face nervously with his fingernail. "We must go, Samuel," he said. "Mrs. Lindstrom was expecting us twenty minutes ago." The man reached out his hand. "Now, come along," he urged.

Samuel nodded and turned to leave although he really didn't want to go. He liked the garden and the cool, shaded patio. He liked the way the tree branches overlapped each other and formed a leafy dome above his head. He liked the lady of the place. She was sad, but beautiful, and although he barely knew her, there was something about her that seemed familiar.

"Just a moment, George," she called. She walked over to the boy and placed her hand on his shoulder. "Samuel," she said, "perhaps you will come again and visit me."

The boy's face brightened, and Lillian saw a sparkle in his blue eyes. "I need someone to help me in the garden, also." She looked at the lawyer with a questioning expression on her face. "What do you think, George? Do you think Adelle would mind sharing this young man?"

George Henly frowned and looked at Lillian for a moment. She was up to something, he thought. "I just hope she will agree to take him in, Lillian. There are others living with her, you know."

Samuel looked down, and Lillian knew his feelings were hurt. She gently lifted his face with her hand and smiled at him. What a handsome boy he was! A little pale perhaps, but quite good-looking, with piercing blue eyes and dark hair. He was tall for a boy his age and thin as a rail. There was something about him that drew him to her heart. "Put his bag down, George," she said. "Go and tell Adelle Lindstrom you have found a home for Samuel."

"But, Lillian!" protested the lawyer. "You, I

mean we had better talk about this before --"

"We will talk about it, George," interrupted the woman. "We'll talk about it in your office tomorrow!" She looked at the lawyer with determination on her face. "Now leave Samuel's bag. I have a guest room off the den that will be just perfect for him."

She pulled the boy to her. "Would you like to stay here, Samuel?" she asked.

"Yes, ma'am," he nodded.

"Good, then. Come and see where you'll be staying."

Samuel looked timidly at the lawyer as he followed Lillian Vanderling to the back door of her house.

George Henly stood there in disbelief. "But, Lillian," he called.

"I'll be at your office at 8:30 tomorrow morning, George," spoke the woman as she ushered the boy into the house.

A thin smile formed on the lips of George Henly. Maybe this wasn't such a bad thing after all, he thought. Adelle Linstrom would be relieved at the news. She had her hands full anyway. Besides, Lillian Vanderling needed someone in her life. Since the death of her husband, she had become somewhat of a recluse. This was sad, for she had always been such an outgoing woman. The Vanderlings had never had children, but it was thought by those who knew them best that they would have been wonderful parents.

Fate is strange, and it has but one partner. That is time. It is only time that will bring fate to its fruition. Perhaps George Henly considered it fate which had brought young Samuel Lively under the caring wings of Lillian Vanderling. Then again, it might have been the simple path of an illusive butterfly. What is known for certain is that on that day the last promise of a young boy's dying mother was fulfilled. . . .

So it was that Samuel Lively made his way up the brick steps and along the walkway towards the great house that had become his home so long ago. He was greeted with smiles and handshakes as he moved towards a podium which was set in the garden where he had first come to know his adopted mother. Together they had tended the garden for many years. Through her he had continued to know the love of a mother, and in him she had found the child she had always wanted.

Samuel talked to the crowd of people that day. He spoke of his life, of how he had first been guided by the advice of his mother and then by the example of Miss Lilly. "She saw something in me that stood apart from my awkwardness," he told the people. "And she loved me for who I was. She believed we all come here with gifts, gifts that should be noticed and nourished."

The sun broke through the clouds then, and a butterfly fluttered about the head of Samuel before lighting upon his shoulder. The crowd responded with chuckles and murmurs, but for a moment Samuel was astonished. He knew the color and design of that butterfly because he had seen it before and followed it to this very place.

Samuel smiled and finished his speech by saying, "Today it is with pride and great joy that, in loving memory of my mother, Lillian Vanderling, I declare this estate The Vanderling School for the Gifted. It is her dream come true."

Later that day, Samuel stood alone on the patio where he had met Lillian. It had not changed. There were the same cobblestones, the great trees towering above him, the fragrance of the flowers in the garden. She had seemed sad that day, long ago, but soon after that day her sadness disappeared. The remainder of her years she spent bringing happiness and opportunity not only to her adopted son but also to others.

Samuel knew that he was part of her joy. He also knew something else. Just before Lillian died, she told her son this: "I saw the word on the page with the crystal rose, and I understood for the first time in my life that a love held within one's heart is but a stifled emotion. Free it, and it will shine in every soul it touches."

Samuel never searched for the crystal rose in his adopted mother's possessions. He knew she had passed it on.

The Marriage

Ellie brushed back the hair from her face. "There, now," she said. "How does that look?"

Janie, her younger sister, held up a little square mirror and answered, "You are beautiful, Ellie. Just look at yourself."

The older girl made a face. "I need something like a flower in my hair. Betty, where's one of those little lavender flowers we saw the other day?"

Betty was already looking around the base of the tree she was standing beside. "Here they are!" she answered, triumphantly, while stooping down and pinching one off at its base. She walked over and placed it in Ellie's hair, just above her left ear. She stood back and looked closely at her friend.

"No, that's not it," she said, shaking her head. "Let's try this." She stepped behind Ellie and, with both hands, pulled the girl's long flowing hair back behind her head. Then she took the white ribbon from her own hair, put it around Ellie's, and tied it into a nice bow. She placed the delicate flower in Ellie's hair at her right temple. "There it is." She smiled. "Hold up the mirror, Janie, and let her see."

Ellie swallowed nervously with excitement as Janie brought up the little mirror, and she nodded agreeably when she saw Betty's work.

"I like it, Betty," she said. "What do you think, Janie?"

The younger girl smiled, "You're just beautiful, Ellie. I swear you are, and if that boy don't think you're the prettiest thing he's ever seen, he ain't got no eyes in his head."

"What time is it, y'all?" Betty asked.

Janie lifted a little gold watch from her dress pocket and answered, "It's four minutes after ten." The pocket watch didn't have a chain on it, and it was somewhat worn, but it kept good time. "That boy'd better get here soon, or we're gonna have to get back to the house. Mama said we best be home by eleven, or we'll miss our ride to town, and we got to see that new Claudette Colbert movie. It's on at the Lee. I just love that woman."

"What's it called?" asked Betty. She had leaned against the giant maple tree.

Janie got a puzzled look on her face. "Well, uh, I think it's called *Flags for You*, or something like that —"

"No, Janie," interrupted Ellie. "It's called *Under Two Flags*, and it has Ronald Coleman in it. Mama likes him, but I don't. I'm partial to Clark Gable."

Betty agreed. "Now, that's a man."

Janie sighed and looked at her watch again.

"Well, if Jack doesn't get here soon, we'll all be staying home today."

Ellie looked up the hill through the woods. She knew he would come. Besides, she hadn't planned on going anywhere that day. She was already where she wanted to be. . . .

Jack Stillman had gotten up early that morning. There were chores to do, and today he had to do them quicker than usual. He had some-place special to go. So when his dad found him out at the chicken house gathering eggs and told him they needed to make a run into town for some lumber, the boy was quietly annoyed.

"How long do you think it'll take, Dad?" he asked, while fumbling with the last egg.

The man picked up on his son's mood and answered, "It won't take long, Son. Why? You catchin' a train or somethin'?"

The boy scooted by his father on his way to the house. "No, sir, ain't no train or nothin'," he called back. "Just got somethin' I want to do, that's all."

John Stillman chuckled as he flung open the hood of the Ford truck. "Well, if Ole Knock About here's got a mind for it, we ought to be back by mid-morning, I reckon." He was talking to himself by then and heard the screen door to the house slam.

Everybody the Stillmans knew was in town that day, and it seemed to Jack that his dad was holding court at every stop. So by the time they finished loading up at the lumberyard, Jack was biting at the bit to get home. John Stillman was a talker, though, and he knew a lot about some things and a little about everything else. Consequently, it didn't take much for him to get into a conversation with friend or stranger. But when Mangus Ruby leaned into the truck and started talking about the price of lumber, a danger alert went off in Jack's brain. He pulled out his watch and saw the time was nine twenty-five. Mangus was rattling on about how you'd better pick out your own two-by-fours or two-by-eights, or they'll load you up with bowed wood, when Jack interrupted, "Excuse me, Mr. Ruby."

Mangus stopped and looked a bit startled.

"Dad, we got to get on home now! Remember?"

John Stillman looked over at his son and saw that the boy was fidgety. He looked back at Mangus and tapped him on the forearm. "Mangus, we got to get on, ole boy. You take it easy, now, you hear?"

Mangus slapped the door of the Ford and pushed away. "Take care, John. Y'all come see us."

John waved and pulled onto the road. "All right, Son," he said. "I'll get you to the church on time if Ole Knock About will cooperate."

Jack didn't say anything, but the comment about getting to the church on time made him a little nervous. He wondered just how intuitive his dad really was.

By the time the Ford pulled into the Stillman driveway, it was almost ten o'clock. John drove the truck to a shady spot under a big red oak and parked it. Jack was halfway to the house when he heard his dad call, "We'll unload her

94

later on."

Jack stopped and turned around. He knew his dad would normally unload the lumber immediately and stack it in the shed, so he couldn't help feeling guilty. "Wait for me, Dad," he called back. "Don't do it on your own."

The man waved his hand at his son. "Get on, now. We'll get to it later."

Jack spun around and opened the screen door. Inside, his mother was baking pies for the church social on Sunday. "Save one for us, Mom," Jack said, as he hurried by her.

"Y'all get the lumber?" she asked.

Jack stopped at the entrance to the hall. "Yes, ma'am." He thumped the door frame nervously. "We'll get it unloaded this afternoon."

Katherine Stillman bent over and placed two more apple pies in the oven. "Where you off to, Son?" she asked, while wiping the sweat from her neck with her apron.

"Goin' down to the river, Mama."

"Well, good. Bring us back a mess of fish for supper."

"I'll try to, Mama." Jack turned and ran through the hall and up the stairs to his room. He heard his mother call after him. "You watch out for copperheads, you hear?"

"Yes, ma'am. I'll watch out for 'em," Jack

called back as he reached into his closet for a clean shirt, white and neatly pressed. He would have to leave the house by the front door because his mother knew he didn't go fishing in his Sunday shirt. He quickly washed his face and combed his hair. He pulled the shirt on, buttoned it, and tucked it into his trousers. Then he looked at himself in the mirror. It was a good day, he thought, while examining his face. No pimples. And for a teenaged boy, that's good. He looked at his watch. It was two minutes past ten.

Jack opened his sock drawer and reached back until his fingers felt the box. He pulled it out and opened it. It wasn't a ring, but it would have to do. And, besides, he could think of no one he'd rather give it to. He closed the box and tucked it into his pants pocket.

He came out of the front door of his house and moved cautiously around towards the shed where he kept his fishing gear. His dad was rummaging around in the barn, so he ran across the dirt driveway and grabbed his fishing rod and tackle box. A minute later, he was entering the woods at the edge of the canteloupe patch. Once he was inside the forest, he ran like hell.

Betty heard him coming first. "Well, I'll be," she said, looking up the hill. "Either that boy's in a hurry to get here, or something awful is after him, Ellie," she remarked.

Ellie smiled and looked at Janie. "See, I knew he'd come."

"What's he totin'?" asked Janie.

No one answered.

The girls just watched as Jack came panting into the small clearing.

"Hi," he said breathlessly. "Sorry I'm a little late."

Ellie smiled shyly. "Hello, Jack."

Janie studied the boy for a moment and said, "Jack, we weren't going on no fishing trip."

"I know," he said, "but Mama wants a mess of fish for supper, and I told her I would try to catch some."

Janie rolled her eyes.

Betty covered her mouth and stifled a giggle.

Ellie took the fishing gear from Jack's hands and placed it on the ground. "Later," she said. "Betty and Janie have to leave by eleven."

"What about you, Ellie?" Janie was making a bouquet of yellow flowers and ferns.

"Not today, Janie. I'm not going to town today."

"Well, are you two sure you want to do this?" asked Betty, as she took her place next to the maple tree.

Jack looked at Ellie. "I'm sure," he said.

"Me, too," responded Ellie.

Janie looked at Betty and lifted the bouquet to her face. "Umm, these smell so sweet." She handed the bouquet to her sister, then took her place beside her.

Jack reached out his hand, and Ellie took it and squeezed it. She was nervous, Jack could tell. Her small hand was cool and damp. "Are you all right, Ellie?" he asked.

"I'm fine," she assured him. Ellie could not believe this was really happening. But she wanted it to happen. Even if it had to be like this. A secret. No one would understand. They would say it was puppy love. They'd call it foolishness and declare that one day she wouldn't feel this way about him. How could teenagers be in love? It couldn't be real. Kid's can't possibly fall in love. Not real love. Taken over by new and profound emotions perhaps, or mere infatuation. But real love? The kind that keeps a man and a woman together for years? Not a chance, people would say. You're too young for such commitment.

Ellie's mind played it all back every day. And still she knew what she felt. It was true and deep love that she had felt for Jack for a long time. And the basis for it was a trusted friendship. He wasn't the handsomest boy in school, and certainly not the smartest, but there were things about him that made him appeal to her in a way no one else could. He was kind and unpretentious, and there was conviction in his heart that made him steadfast. Jack Stillman was quite unlike any other person Ellie had ever known. He would not blow away. Not by storm or temptation.

Ellie knew that she loved Jack, and she longed to become one with his heart and soul.

For Jack, it was very simple. He had loved Ellie since the first time he saw her, and he knew that he would love her for the rest of his life, no matter what.

Doves cooed in the pines along the hilltop, and the cicadas were calling, when Betty spoke up.

"Are y'all ready?"

"We're ready," answered Jack.

Betty began. "We're here today, in the presence of God and nature, to unite Jack and Ellie in Holy Matrimony. Because of the small-mindedness of the world, we come together in secrecy. But our hearts are true and our pact strong, and the words spoken this day, and the commitment made, will remain with us always. Let this ground be sacred, and the shadows of the forest dance with joy in the hearts of these two people. Let this love stand as strong as the maple tree that towers above them."

Having said these words, Betty looked at Jack. "Do you wish to speak, Jack?" she asked.

Jack looked into the eyes of his young bride and said, "Ellie, you have entered my heart and soul, and I will love you forever." He opened her hand and placed in it a small wooden box.

She opened it and saw what it contained was beautiful beyond words. Tears filled her eyes, and her hands trembled. Softly she spoke. "As the heavens are endless, so will be my love for you."

Jack felt that his very soul was drawn into her blue eyes. Heaven could not be so sweet as this, he thought.

For a time no one spoke. Finally, with a nod of her head, Janie urged Betty to say something.

"Then, with the power invested in me by God, a sane mind and – and –," the girl looked around her and touched the bark of the maple tree before continuing, "and this maple tree, I pronounce you man and wife. You may kiss your bride, Jack."

Janie put her hand to her lips and smiled.

Betty feigned looking up into the tree

branches, but Ellie leaned into the arms of her love and was oblivious to everything else around her.

Later, as the two young lovers sat cuddled beneath the maple tree, they spoke quietly.

"Do you really think they'll keep quiet about it, Ellie?"

"Without a doubt, honey," replied the bride. "If Reverend Cook knew that his precious daughter performed her first wedding ceremony today, he'd preach her the hardest sermon she'd ever hear. And Janie. Well, Janie will always honor the pact we made."

"I want to tell the world, Ellie. But I know what would happen."

"I know, Jack. I feel the same way."

"I love you, Ellie," Jack kissed her lips.

"And I love you."

Jack looked at his watch and jumped to his feet.

"What's wrong, Jack?"

"Well, there's another promise I've got to fulfill today."

"What's that?"

"I've got to catch a mess of fish for dinner, or somebody might be wonderin' what I did out here today."

Ellie laughed and stood up. "Let's go,

then," she said, as Jack picked up the tackle box and fishing rod.

In a few minutes, they were sitting side by side on the bank of the river, and the fish were biting like crazy. Plans were being made, and hopes shared. Forever seemed as endless as a clear blue sky, and yet dark clouds were looming in the distance. . . .

For three and a half years, Jack and Ellie continued to see one another as often as possible, and they were sensible about their situation, not wishing to become too obvious to their folks, or worse, bringing anything that even touched on shame to the ones they loved.

But a day came when Ellie's family moved away, and two hearts were broken. Their parting was the saddest day of their young lives. Of course, promises were made. But promises are dependent on more than the commitment of two hearts. Chance and circumstance also play their parts in what is to be and what is not.

Finally, what their hearts would not allow, the hatred of men accomplished. The world became engulfed in the flaming chaos of war, as Hitler and his Nazis turned their wicked will and power towards world dominance.

Fathers and sons and husbands and brothers took up arms to bring a halt to a hell on earth.

Many were lost forever, and some were presumed to be lost, until, to the joy of some and the sorrow of others, they showed themselves again. Jack was one of these, for after months in the blood and mire of battle, he fell into the morbid shadows of a prison camp and disappeared seemingly from the face of the earth.

Ellie was stunned because she knew that the love of her life was gone forever.

But young hearts are resilient, and with the will to live, so comes the need to love again.

Before the war ended, and two years after she last heard from Jack, Ellie was married in a church and began a new life. She learned of Jack's survival soon after the war ended. Janie had heard about Jack through Betty, who had become one of the first female ministers in Virginia. She had a church in the town near where Jack's family lived, and had seen him and spoken to him. It was Betty who told Jack of Ellie's marriage.

Ellie could not believe her lot in life, for now she would always be torn between the man she had come to love and the one she would always love.

For Jack it was equally hard, except for one difference. He had given his heart and soul once, and he knew he did not have them to give again.

So he lived in the house with his mother and father and farmed the land and slowly mended mentally and physically from the ravages of the war. And as long as Betty was in town, he kept up the best he could with Ellie and with where life had taken her. He knew about her children and her miscarriage. He knew about her husband's promotions, and he knew that he was a good man. He knew that Ellie had become a nurse, and he wasn't surprised because she used to make over him so much. Any little scratch justified immediate attention, even when they were children.

Ellie's life had turned out all right, and so he was happy for her. There was a part of him that always wanted to go to her, to see her again, to hear her voice. But there was a greater part that stilled his desires. Perhaps that was the greatest love of all, to sacrifice one's own desires for the well-being of another.

Betty had a church in Lynchburg after so many years, and Jack still heard from her occasionally. Good old Betty. As faithful to a friend as she was to the Lord. And her faithfulness was a two-way street. One to Jack, and the other to Ellie.

For Ellie also knew of Jack's life, and the sacrifice of his heart. . . .

Years passed, and by 1987, the small town where Ellie had grown up had become a bustling hub. There were colleges and industry and many new businesses, as well as old family operations.

"Look at the lake, Janie," Ellie pointed.

Janie leaned forward in the car and looked out the window. There were people sunbathing on grassy terraces. "They've opened it up to the public. Didn't it belong to the Jamersons, Betty?"

Betty cleared her throat. "Yes, they donated it to the town a while back. But y'all just wait. You're not going to believe Jack's place."

Ellie felt Janie's hand on her shoulder. "Are you nervous, Sis?"

Ellie reached back and patted her younger sister's hand. "I'm excited, Janie," she answered. "And I think it's going to be just fine."

"He looks good," Betty offered. "Farming suited him, Ellie." She looked over at Ellie in the passenger's seat. "He has a slight limp. They say he got torn up right bad in the War. But he's healthy as a horse."

Betty took Ellie's hand and squeezed it. "I'm just so happy, Ellie," she said.

Ellie smiled. "Me, too, Betty. Me, too." She looked out the window and thought about life and how living it can be like a ride on a roller coaster. It takes you up and down and then around, and, somehow, it ends where it begins. Her heart had been on that roller coaster. A strange mixture of happiness and tragedy. Breathtaking highs and gut-wrenching lows. The despair of losing Jack and then the pain of knowing he was alive, but lost to her. Her marriage and her beautiful children. And then the loss of her husband. There was a reason for it all. There is always a reason. She had felt that all of her life.

Ellie looked over at Betty. She was such a dear friend. Had it not been for her, she wouldn't be here now, she thought. There wouldn't be another beginning. Good and true Betty.

"Another lake?" asked Janie.

"That's Jack's lake, ladies!" Betty turned left on a freshly graveled road. "He dammed up that stream below the big maple tree and formed his own lake. Has a pontoon, a boathouse, and even a little cabin."

"Sounds like you're in for it, Sis," laughed Janie.

Ellie saw the farmhouse in the distance. It looked the same, but with a fresh coat of paint. Sometimes you can go back, she thought.

Jack was standing in the shade of the oak tree when the car pulled to a stop. He was on the driver's side of the car, so Betty got the first hug and kiss. "Hello, you old sweet thing," she teased.

"You're looking good, Betty," he laughed.

Janie stepped out of the back seat of the car and hurried over to him. He squeezed her tight. "Little Janie. Let me look at you." He shook his head. "I can't believe you grew up to be so pretty. You were such a ratty little thing." Jack put his arms up in mock defense.

Janie laughed out loud and rolled her eyes. "I was a real late bloomer."

Ellie stepped out of the car next, and Jack stood still. His lips parted, and he said her name.

"We'll be down at the tree, dear," said Betty. She touched his arm and motioned for Janie to follow her. Janie looked back at her sister and winked.

"Hello, Jack." Ellie's voice was shaky. She didn't want to cry, but she felt it coming. Here she was, after fifty years. That's a long time to imagine what you might say or do. There he was, tall and tan, and looking younger than his years. He had not sent her any pictures of himself since they had been writing. But the letters were always there. Every week, for almost a year. It was as if she had known him all her life. She knew in her heart that she had.

Jack walked around the front of the car and took her in his arms.

She pressed her face against his chest and wept softly. "I was afraid I would never see you again," she cried. She felt his body shaking, and she knew he was crying, also.

"I love you, Ellie," he whispered. He reached down and kissed her, and half a century between them melted away. Their hearts were back to where they had begun.

She wiped the tears from his face. "Are you sure, Jack?" she asked.

"I've always been sure, Ellie." He put his arm around her waist and led her away from the car. "Are you sure?" he asked. "You know, I'm not the young fella you once knew."

Ellie patted his chest. "He's in there." She stopped and turned towards the one she had fallen in love with so long ago, the man she had lost and then found again. With conviction in her voice, she looked into his eyes and said, "I have only been really sure of one other thing in my life, Jack. And that was when I married you the first time."

He knew she meant that. There was no doubt. "Well, come then," he said. "We'll take Ole Knock About." Jack strode over to the shed and pulled open the double doors.

Ellie was amazed.

Jack opened the truck door and helped her

in. "Dad made me promise to keep her going," he explained with a grin. He started up the engine, and it purred smoothly. Then they were off.

By the time they came to the maple tree, Betty and Janie were ready.

Ellie marveled at how the maple had withstood the years.

"Amazing, isn't it?" commented Jack. "She's been hit by lightning a couple of times, but refuses to die."

"That's because this is sacred ground," explained Betty. "Remember?"

Everybody remembered.

"Now, let's see," muttered Betty. "I think I stood right about here." She took her place. "And, Janie, dear, you were right there," she pointed.

Janie had gathered some little yellow wild flowers and made a bouquet with ferns. She breathed in their fragrance. "Sweet as ever," she said.

Jack and Ellie took their places under the maple, as doves cooed in pines and cicadas called out from high in the trees. And a secret little moment in time was repeated. One that could be mentioned in the local paper this time around.

Later, two happy people sat in chairs and looked out over a shimmering lake.

"Couldn't give you much of a honeymoon back then, Ellie," Jack confessed.

"I didn't expect one."

"Well, you know, I'd like to visit Europe again without a gun in my hand, or one pointed at my head. How 'bout it?"

Ellie laughed, "I'd like that, Jack. I've never been to Europe." She touched her wedding ring and leaned her head against Jack's shoulder.

A long moment of silence passed between the two lovers.

Then Jack kissed Ellie's forehead. "What did you do with the rose?" he asked.

"I passed it along after a while, like you told me to do."

"Did you get anything from it, Ellie?"

Ellie remembered the crystal rose and what it had meant to her so long ago. And then she answered her husband, "Yes, Jack. I got you again."

Jack took her small hand in his and spoke softly, "You always had me, Ellie. Always."

The Poet

Night after night he sat at the table in his dimly lit apartment and voiced the words of his heart with a pen and paper. Alone, he would seldom open his mouth to speak or even whisper for fear that hearing his own voice would remind him of things he did not wish to remember.

Occasionally he would stand and pace back and forth over worn floor boards that creaked beneath his weight, until, suddenly, the word or phrase that he wanted would come to him, and he would sit and write again. Then he would lean back in his wooden chair with its ragged seat and sip tea from a tin cup. It was strong, with a touch of honey. That's the way he preferred it.

If there was a full moon or a star-filled night, he would hear the howling of dogs at the edge of town. First one, and then an annoying chorus. He would go to his window and will them to stop. Sometimes they did. He would sit and write again -- or think about words and phrases.

During the daytime, he smiled and spoke. He was a waiter at a cafe a couple of blocks from his room. He liked to see new faces, so the cafe was a good place to be. He would take orders and answer questions about where a specific place might be found. Tourists loved the small village where he lived.

"It's so quaint," they would say. "Isn't it just lovely to live in such a place?" they would ask.

And he would always say, "Oh, yes, it is."

They did not know where he had come from. They did not know anything about him. To them, he was only a waiter. But in his heart he was something more. He was a poet. A published one, at that. *Poet's Monthly* had published his work. Two of his poems had been in that magazine. He had even won a national poetry contest. One hundred dollars and publication in *River*

Times. That was a New York magazine, and it boasted 20,000 readers. Some literary agents had contacted him through the mail after that, and for a while, he was excited – until he was told, "They'll take your money, and you won't get much for it in return." He had heard that from an intoxicated writer. The man had said he had written a book, but the poet had never heard of it although he read a lot. Reading was his escape.

When he was a child, it was the only way out of hell. In books, he could sail with pirates on the open seas, or romance a young maiden. He could travel and see the world, if only in his mind's eye. In books, he had courage, whereas in life he had none. There were scars in his heart, and some on his skin. He had not ever been bad, only born into something bad, but children will blame themselves for things beyond their control. Things they have little or nothing to do with. Painful things. They were in his heart, and sometimes in his poems although he didn't realize that. Writing was his passion, and he painted his sadness with beautiful words. He wrote of spring mornings and dew-laden petals, of waterfalls and streaks of sunlight that shone through forest canopies like golden fingers from heaven. For everything wrong, he could make something right with his words.

There were those times when the words would not come to blanket his pain, and scars that would not heal throbbed like crimson welts on his heart. The circle seemed endless until one day something profound in effect occurred.

It began with a stranger's voice. "Are you the poet?" asked the old man who sat alone at a corner table.

"Yes, I am," answered the poet. He had seen the old gentleman for the past week or so as he would amble in at about the same time each day and occupy his favorite chair in the corner by the front window. There he would have his coffee and read the paper and look up occasionally to notice a passerby. Sometimes he would smile, and always he was pleasant. The cafe was practically empty that morning, so the young poet sat down on the edge of a chair opposite the old man. "How did you know?" he asked, as the man raised his coffee cup to his lips.

A car horn blared outside, and both men looked out the window to see the reason for it. They watched as a calico cat scuttled out of harm's way, finding sanctuary beneath one of the round tables which sat along the sidewalk just beyond the window. It hunched there, frightened for the moment, but quickly it regained its composure and walked lightly up the sidewalk.

"The cat has a limp," the old man commented.

"Yes," agreed the poet. "It's probably been hit before."

The old man nodded his head and returned to his coffee. When he put his cup down, he spoke. "My name's Arlie Gunner, and I live a ways up Roddy's Branch. You ever heard of it?"

"Yes, sir, I have."

"Well, I retired a while back, and now I just fish and hunt and read a lot."

The poet could see the old fellow was a man of the outdoors. His face was tanned, with age lines that looked as if they had been etched by the wind. His hands were a bit gnarled and calloused.

The old man continued, "I saw your picture and read about you in *River Times*. Congratulations on winning."

"Thank you," responded the surprised poet.

"I liked your poem a lot," the man continued. "You describe things real good. Like you know something about them. I think you've traveled some. Am I right?"

The poet didn't see any harm in answering the question and, besides, he was becoming intrigued by Arlie Gunner. "Well, yes, Mr. Gunner," he responded. "I've been around some, and I do love the hills and the woods."

"I knew it," the old man chuckled. "I figured you were cut that way. By the way, call me Arlie."

The poet smiled, "All right, Arlie." He was aware that the name had a ring to it. A friendly ring.

"Do you hunt and fish any, Son?" the man asked.

"No, sir," answered the poet. The question was normal enough, except for that word at the end. No one had ever called him that. He wasn't so sure how it made him feel, but he explained, "I can't hurt anything, Arlie. I guess I just don't have it in me."

The old man shrugged. "Well, I can understand that, Son. It's not for everyone. I just like to eat fish and venison, and there's not a critter I know of that'll jump in the skillet on its own."

The poet laughed. "I guess not."

"That article told some things about you, but it didn't mention your folks. Got any?" Arlie Gunner finished his coffee and placed his cup in its saucer.

The poet was a little uncomfortable now, and he looked behind him at the door. No one had come in, but he wished someone would.

The old man noticed the body language of the poet, and he realized he'd touched upon an awkward subject. He wasn't surprised. He had read the young man's other writings and had gathered as much. Arlie Gunner, you see, was a man with great insight. When he wasn't hunting or fishing or walking about in the mountains, he was studying folks and talking with them. He had been that way all his life. Always wanting to converse with others and never satisfied to know just a few. There was a drive in Arlie that he could not, or would not, deny. He wanted to learn something from every soul he met, and he was willing to give something in return.

"I don't have any folks, Arlie." The poet didn't understand why he was compelled to answer the question, but something in him wanted the old man to know. In his heart, it was not a lie.

Arlie looked at the young man and then down at his empty cup. "Well, I'm alone, too, Son," he said quietly, as if he understood all too well. "You know, I'd like to extend an invitation to you to come visit me up on Roddy's Branch this Sunday, and I'll show you a pretty waterfall hardly anyone knows about. How 'bout it?" Arlie waited for an answer.

The poet clicked his fingernails on the table and moved nervously in his chair. "Well, I don't know, Arlie," he began.

Arlie waved his hand. "Listen," he interceded, "you just think about it and feel free to come on up if you want to. Sundays, I go to church in the glen, but I'll be home by noon." He rose from his chair and tucked his paper under his arm. "Think about it, Son," he said. "It might be fodder for your poetry. Who knows?"

The poet stood up and shook the old man's hand. "I will," he promised. "If I can."

Arlie smiled and moved around the table. He patted the young man on the shoulder and left.

The poet watched as the old man crossed the street, stepped into an old truck, and disappeared around the corner. He thought about Arlie Gunner for the rest of the day, and that night he made a decision. The day after tomorrow he would take a little walk up to Roddy's Branch and see where his new friend lived.

It rained on Saturday, but Sunday was a diamond day. The sun was shining brightly, with not a cloud in the sky, when the poet took the final leg up Roddy's Branch and rounded a curve in the narrow road. Leaves were just beginning to turn, as the early chill of fall was in the air. The walk up had been pleasant, and more than once the poet had sat among mossy stones along the trickling stream and listened for words in its quiet song.

Arlie was right, he thought. There was fodder for his poems up here. When he finally walked into the yard of Arlie's house, he felt immediately at home. The house was a log structure with a rusty tin roof. On the front porch there were two rocking chairs, with a half whiskey barrel between them, turned up for a table. Wind chimes hung from thick beams, and a faint stream of smoke swirled up from a fieldstone chimney. The place was tidy. Arlie's truck was parked under a shed off to the side of the cabin.

The front door opened as the poet neared the porch steps, and out walked Arlie, with a grin on his face and a steaming cup in his hand. "Glad you could make it up, Son." He was wearing a thin flannel shirt with the sleeves rolled up to his elbows, old brown corduroys, and leather suspenders. Leather boots laced up to the knees completed his attire and made the poet think of a picture he'd seen once of a character out of the Maine woods.

"Hello, Arlie," greeted the poet. "I like your place." He stepped up on the wide plank porch and reached out his hand.

Arlie took it and shook it with a firm grip. "Come on in, Son," he said. "Coffee?"

"No, thanks." The young man stepped into the cabin.

Arlie moved back towards the kitchen area. "Let me put this cup and some things away and then we'll be off. Just make yourself at home."

The poet looked around the room. It was like stepping into a storybook. There were deer mounts on the walls, and a stuffed bear standing over in a corner of the room. A rack on the wall held a couple of rifles and a double-barreled shotgun. An old flintlock long rifle hung on the wall above a massive fireplace mantel. Ragged, but beautiful, Indian rugs lay over wide worn floorboards, and there were paintings of wildlife scenes everywhere on the walls. A bookcase, with its many shelves loaded with books, lined the back wall off to the right of the kitchen, and there was a desk holding stacks of papers and a black Underwood typewriter. A wall behind a soft leather sofa was covered in pictures. The poet recognized Arlie in some of them. Other faces looked familiar, too, but he didn't know why. There were hunting pictures, where men stood displaying their kills, and photographs of Arlie as a young soldier. In one photograph, he posed, smiling, arm-in-arm with an attractive young woman. There were no pictures of children.

The floor creaked, and the poet turned around. Arlie was wearing his hat. He nodded his head at the photographs on the wall. "There're some good memories there. I've been a lucky man." He turned and walked to the door. "Well, come on, there's a waterfall to see."

With that, the poet followed the old man out the door into a world he thought he knew. . .

Over the next few months he came to know the old man as a dear friend. Never before in the young poet's life had he shared so much with one person. He loved to hear Arlie's stories. Also, they talked about books and writers. Sunday became their day together, and if the weather was fine, they would walk the hills. The older man would entertain his young friend with tales and folklore. On Sundays, when the weather was bad, they would sit by the hearth and read or talk. Each man had found in the other something he had always longed for. The older man knew what it was he had gained; but the poet, for all of his joy, could not imagine that he was worthy of the gift given him.

So they continued, the old man and the poet, and somehow, as they grew closer, a oneness was born in their hearts.

The young poet's writings became better as his spirit was lifted from the shackles of his youth. The words and phrases that had once trickled through his heart now came in volumes. There were not enough hours in the day to harness all the beauty of his thoughts. He wrote as he had never written before, and always he shared his writing with the old man.

One day as they sat among mossy stones below the waterfall, Arlie Gunner handed the poet a small box. His hand shook as the young man accepted his gift. Arlie swallowed and cleared his throat. The poet began to lift the lid of the worn wooden box when the old man stopped him. "I was given this by someone that I hardly knew," he explained. "That person told me that, some day when I understood it, I should pass it on to another." Arlie looked up at the waterfall for a moment and then back at the face of the poet. "I want you to take it and do the same." He reached over and tapped the lid of the box with a gnarled finger. "I don't think there's any magic in that box that's not already in all of us. It's just a reminder of the only thing that makes you complete." Arlie put his hand on the poet's shoulder. "I'll be leaving soon. It's time. But I want you to know that you've been like a son to me."

The young poet looked down at the box in his hand. There was enormous sorrow in his heart.

Arlie felt it and spoke. "You're a fine and gifted young man, and I know that someday the world will read your words. I'm honored that you've shared them with me. . . ."

When Arlie Gunner left his place on Roddy's Branch, the young poet moved into his cabin and there he lived and wrote for many years.

And the world did read his words, just as Arlie had said it would.

Epilogue

After my dreams ceased, I felt the need in my heart to pass along the crystal rose. And so I did.

There is no doubt in my mind that it still moves from hand to hand, and heart to heart, always the reminder that the wealth of the soul is measured by one thing, and one thing only, *Love* . . .

Forever

TITLES BY FRANCIS EUGENE WOOD

The Wooden Bell (A Christmas Story)

The Legend of Chadega and the Weeping Tree

Wind Dancer's Flute

The Angel Carver

The Fodder Milo Stories

The Nipkins

These books and others are available through the author's
web site at http://tipofthemoon.com